A Fatal
Exception

A Fatal Exception

Scott Finlay

CHAPTER 1

Chicago, a nice enough piece of concrete and glass, but in the winter it's a real pile of frozen dung, or at least that's what the organics would say. The cold didn't bother Seven though aside from a bit of stiffness in his bearings. Seven's fleshy counterparts were already beginning to complain about the early November chill, murmuring begrudgingly about the encroaching icy season.

Chicago was a figurative gold mine for private investigators like Seven. The crime rate was surpassed only by the level of corruption in its legal system, and the citizens trusted the personal touch more than what their hard-earned tax money paid for. The city wasn't what it used to be, or at least that's what they said; Seven couldn't really remark otherwise on account of the fact he was technically only six years old. He could, however, cite nearly fourteen thousand sources describing the near exponential growth in reported crimes over the past decade. Not that the rest of the country was really much better.

Seven sat motionless behind the disorderly mahogany desk in the dark office of the Sinclair Detective Agency way up on the 92nd floor of the Ace Tower. This was how he spent most days while waiting for a client to walk through his doors which he always kept unlocked while he was present. Seven was a being of simple needs, requiring no food or water, no toilet, no entertainment. He simply waited, connecting himself to the net in order to keep up-to-date with the world news and to drop little advertisements onto websites which failed his security probes.

It was 9:32 a.m. on a dreary Tuesday morning when the bright white LED lighting suddenly flipped on as the motion sensor in the back corner of the office detected the opening of the front door. As if connected to the same sensors, the backlight behind Seven's eyes flickered on giving them a dull blue glow.

"Welcome, what can I do for you?" stated Seven in an artificially gruff, nasally voice.

"Oh, hello," said the man in a startled tone, still holding the brass doorknob. "I wasn't sure anyone was home. The lights were out. This is the Sinclair Detective Agency, right?"

"Sure is," replied Seven. "Why don't you take a seat." He held out an upturned silver palm towards the dusty, green upholstered chair opposite his desk.

The man in his shabby, brown tweed suit hesitated for a moment but then closed the door behind him and sat down. Seven judged him to be perhaps mid-to-late twenties; it was always difficult to tell with organics as there were so many unknown factors which accelerated or decelerated the aging process.

"So tell me, what can I do for you?"

"I, uh, I have a bit of a predicament and I was hoping that Mr. Sinclair could help me resolve it. I heard that this agency is quite good with more…technical problems."

"Mr. Sinclair isn't available at the moment, but I'm more than capable of receiving the initial case summary." Seven paused for a moment to see how his client reacted. More often than not they spewed out a few words of vacillation before stating they would return some other time when Vic Sinclair was available. Usually they didn't come back.

As expected, this man hesitated, but after a span of about 800 milliseconds he nodded and said, "Yes, of course."

"Excellent, then before we begin just a short matter of business: how did you hear about us?"

"Oh," replied the tired-looking blonde man who had clearly forgotten to shave this morning sounding a little surprised and amused. "Well it's odd really. I was browsing news on the Windy City Tribune when I stumbled upon a text blurb in the article which sounded like a quote from a satisfied customer. It almost looked like it was part of the actual article."

"Good," stated Seven, already beginning to factor that information into his campaigns. He always utilized any opportunity to fine-tune his little cross-site scripting escapades. "Now to the matter of your predicament. How can we help you today?"

"Hmm, I'm not sure where to start," replied the prospective client with a shy smile. "I've never done something like this before."

"How about with your name," suggested Seven. The man's name didn't really interest him, but a name can nevertheless be a valuable piece of information. "And after that just start from the beginning."

"Right, of course! Where are my manners?" said the client sounding embarrassed like a man realizing he had forgotten to observe the standard rules of social engagement. "My name is Ethan, Ethan Willis."

"Well, Mr. Willis—"

"Please, call me Ethan," cut in the young man.

"Ethan, then. I'm Seven Sinclair, but you can call me Seven." Ethan smiled like a school brat who just realized he can make a fart joke out of his new teacher's name.

"A pleasure to make your acquaintance, Seven," he said extending his hand to shake. When Seven returned the gesture, handing him his silver, metallic extremity, Ethan flinched slightly, unnoticeable to the human eye, but detectable by the android.

"So," continued Mr. Willis thoughtfully, "I suppose my trouble is quite simple really. Basically, until yesterday morning I possessed a sizeable sum of money—cryptocurrency to be precise. Yesterday morning when I opened my computer to check my balance it was suddenly zero!"

"Which cryptocurrency?" Cryptocurrencies were a dime a dozen these days, new ones with increasingly silly names were popping up on a near daily basis.

"Bitbucks."

"One of the more stable ones," stated Seven. He knew it was a pointless comment but Vic had taught him that it made the clients feel more comfortable when you added small bits of validation here and there. The instant he uttered the words he registered the desired effect in the man's demeanor as the young man's facial muscles relaxed ever so slightly.

"Yeah, it's basically my entire fortune. I own a small startup and basically all my base capital came from this sum. I don't know what I'm going to do now without it." His voice cracked slightly and, in a whiney tone, he continued, "I took all the right precautions, I thought. I kept my wallet encrypted and backed up."

"What kind of sum are we talking about?" asked Seven.

"300 thousand," moaned Ethan like a groom mourning his dying bride.

Seven produced an artificial whistling sound without moving his steel lips. With that conversion rate he could have started up a whole chain. He wondered what a man of such wealth was doing wearing such a shabby rag of a suit.

"Why don't you go to the police with this?" asked the detective.

"I, uh…everything I say is under client privilege right?"

"Correct. What you say here stays between us."

Ethan sighed lightly and explained, "Well, the thing is, if I go to the authorities it puts a bit of a spotlight on those funds, and I didn't exactly report any of it to the IRS."

"Ah hah," stated Seven. Yet another tax evader. It was no wonder the income tax rates had swollen so fat. Even the president himself had gotten caught up in the middle of a tax fraud scandal three years ago. It didn't stop him from getting reelected. "In that case let's see what we can do for you."

"I brought the computer with, does that help?"

"It sure does, let's have a look."

Ethan reached into the inside pocket of his tweed jacket and withdrew a small tablet PC which he activated and handed to the detective.

Seven scrutinized its exterior briefly, noting minor scratches on the screen and the size and model, already forming educated predictions about its inner components. Within milliseconds, he had already downloaded the technical specifications. Without even bothering to look at the interface, he flipped open a small compartment on his wrist and pulled out one of many wires and plugged it into the jack at the bottom of the device.

"Hmm," said Seven after a moment. He had learned that humans were impatient, and such noises were helpful indicators that he was still processing.

"What is it?" asked Mr. Willis excitedly. "Did you find something?"

The time it had taken him to formulate and verbalize his inquiry had been more than enough for the detective to finish his scans. "There's a good chance that whoever stole your money left you something in its place."

"What do you mean?"

"There's a rootkit on this device, a type of stealth malware, and it was installed two days ago. It's possible that someone could have used this to transmit a copy of your private key."

"Can you find out who did it?"

9

"The virus is still transmitting," stated Seven. "I've reversed the IP address and it seems to be originating from right here in the city, so I'd be willing to bet this was a targeted attack."

"You reversed the IP? When did you do that?" Ethan narrowed his eyes and looked at the metal man with bewilderment.

"Just now."

The young man's face softened again as he said, "Oh right, you talk so unusually for a robot that for a minute there I almost forgot I'm not talking to a real person." Vic would have smacked him for a comment like that, client or not.

Seven continued with his business, unfazed. "It looks like the IP is registered to Orion Industries Inc. Does that mean anything to you?"

Mr. Willis placed his chin in his hand and thought for a moment. Slowly he said, "Hmm, yes. I mean, of course I know the company, who doesn't, but now that you mention it, I have some idea who might have had something against me.

"You see, as I said I own a small startup called Speculo, and I don't want to sound immodest, but we're about to completely revolutionize the world of matter replication. The catch is that we only have a prototype right now and to really mass produce it we need a rare element called ultranium, and Orion Industries is the only major supplier in the country."

"Orion Industries is one of the major players in matter replication technology," stated Seven. "I suppose they weren't very enthusiastic to sell once they heard what it was for."

"Exactly, but I already arranged a deal with the board and about half a dozen executives over the past six months where they would sell Speculo what it needs in exchange for exclusive distribution rights for the first five years. Everything seemed to be aligned until the order landed on the desk of Miles Grayson, one of the top executives over there.

"He declined our order, and when I went to visit him last week it got pretty heated." A bit bashfully he added, "I...may have let myself get a bit carried away."

"And you think this Mr. Grayson is behind your missing funds?"

"The last thing he said to me before security escorted me out of his office was: 'I'm going to personally make sure Speculo never gets is feet off the ground'."

CHAPTER 2

The detective interviewed his client for nearly two hours, but obtained next to nothing worthy of any note. He had expected as much, but he tried to be painstakingly thorough with all his clients. He had learned it from Vic that the clients were often tightlipped, and the details needed to be pried from their minds in the same way you pry open a sticky window. It was a concept which made little sense to Seven given that the customers came of their own free will, but he had nevertheless found it to be true.

During the course of his interview, Seven had spawned a thread to run in his mind's background to gather whatever intel was available on the web about Mr. Miles Grayson. It seemed the man of just over 42 years had steadily risen in the ranks, starting as a lowly business analyst 19 years earlier and climbing over the tattered bodies of his fellow galley rowers until he finally reached what would likely be the zenith of his career as the CFO of Orion Industries just three years ago.

Seven found no evidence that Mr. Grayson possessed any aptitude in the realm of technology, and found it unlikely that the man would have any need for Mr. Willis's money. In any case, the client had indicated a deep suspicion, and the executive's threat couldn't be ignored.

Seven decided he wasn't likely to get any further through simple data mining, so once he had completed his conversation with Ethan Willis, he donned his tan trench coat and brown felt hat and set off to pay a visit to the devil himself.

Outside the Ace Tower where Seven lived and worked, it had grown dark and dreary despite the young hour. About 30 minutes earlier it had begun to rain, one of those cold late autumn rains that made your teeth chatter to the rhythm of the water drops against the pavement. The roads were still bustling with cars and the sidewalks were littered with unhappy people shuffling by with their collars up and their hands thrust deep in their pockets. For a moment Seven thought they looked rather robotic themselves with their stiff limbs, walking on autopilot so they could keep their heads down. Seven wondered if Vic would have laughed at the observation if he had been around. The android found humor a difficult concept to grasp.

The detective approached the curb, raising one metal hand to hail a cab. Instantly one of the many sleek, grey pods separated itself from the herd and drifted over to where Seven stood. The word 'Antifa' was graffitied in large red bubble letters on the door which swiveled open to allow Seven to climb inside the pilotless vehicle.

The hatch closed itself behind him and the indigo interior lighting became the only source of illumination besides the glow of the detective's own eyes. The outside world was only faintly visible through the blackened windows.

"Please state your destination," requested a calm, soothing female voice.

"216 West Jackson Boulevard," replied Seven.

"Please provide your payment instrument," demanded the machine gently.

Seven pulled a plastic card from his pocket, speckled with microchips and metallic contacts and labeled with the name, Victor Sinclair. It was Vic's credit card which Seven was forced to use because the law wouldn't allow him one of his own. He placed the card on the sensor beside the seat.

"Thank you Mr. Sinclair. Please fasten your seatbelt."

After complying, the vehicle slowly drove sideways towards the flow of traffic and merged itself back into the stream, zooming along. About 15 minutes later it pulled back out and dropped him off at the foot of the 142-storey Orion Center, trying to poke a hole in the ozone layer with its lightning rod.

As Seven approached the shiny, modern glass entryway, he was scrutinized by a beefy, steroidal security guard with black tribal tattoos all around his neck, wearing a black suit which looked like it was about to burst at the seams. The guard glared at the android as if somehow Seven would be the suspicious one. The bouncer rotated his head as Seven walked by, but made no move to bar his entry.

Inside, from the high marble ceiling, hung six gaudy crystal chandeliers which glowed brightly with unnaturally white light, leaving little rainbows to decorate the tan marble walls and floor. Seven cut across the way to seek out the reception desk which was manned by a white, plastic-plated gynoid.

"Hello, how can I help you today?" she asked with an unconvincingly artificial enthusiasm, cocking her head to one side with a faint mechanical sound.

"I'd like to speak to Mr. Grayson," replied Seven, making his voice a little gruffer than usual, perhaps in an unconscious attempt to differentiate himself from his peer.

"I'm sorry, Mr. Grayson is very busy, but you can leave your name and business and I'll see if he has any room in his schedule." The fembot tilted her head again and put on a fake smile.

"Tell him a detective is here to talk to him about the financial ruin of Speculo," replied Seven. It was a risky tactic, but he hoped that the truth would be enough to pique the man's curiosity in this case.

The white robot froze for about two minutes, during which time Seven assumed she was telephoning with the executive internally, though he couldn't hear any of the conversation she was transmitting or receiving. Finally, she said, "Mr. Grayson will see you right away."

CHAPTER 3

Sophie Harper anxiously paced the floor of her three by three meter office on the 23rd floor of the Orion Center the way she always did before she had to do something which made her nervous. Quite a lot of things made her nervous, but today's culprit was a particularly ferocious beast. Because her manager had called in sick that morning, she would have to personally deliver her report to the head honcho.

Sophie hated it when she had to see Mr. Grayson. Not only when she had to speak to him, but just the sight of the man made her feel sick to her stomach. She couldn't really explain why she felt this way, perhaps just a general fear of authority, or perhaps it had to do with the man's character. All she knew was that she was not looking forward to the task at hand.

"You can do this Soph," she encouraged herself with a quavering voice. She took a deep breath and counted to three, the way her therapist had instructed. "You're going to just walk right in there and hand it to him and when he reads it maybe you'll even get that promotion you've been waiting for." She doubted it though. She didn't doubt the quality of her work, she knew her report was top-notch, but she had come to expect the lack of appreciation.

The young woman of 26 years walked over to her desk, picked up her half empty coffee mug, and chugged the remainder of the black drink. She had been working since 6 a.m. as usual, and she expected to be in the office until around 9 p.m. These days she lived on that liquid dirt which they brewed in the pot down the hallway.

Finally, with all the resolve she could muster, she slammed the yellow mug on the table, wincing at the sound it made, and with a shaky hand she picked up one of the disposable tablets stacked in her outbox.

The young analyst balled her fists and walked down the brightly lit hallway until she reached the elevator. She reached out to press the up button, but her hand came to a halt just before the little grey square, unable to bring herself to press it. It was almost as if the button and her finger were both the negatively charged ends of a magnet, repelling each other with natural force. Finally, she closed her eyes and uttered a pitiful whining sound like a pouting dog before jamming her forefinger into the button.

Ding! Sounded the elevator almost instantly, causing Sophie to jump.

The shiny metal doors opened to reveal a tall android wearing a brown hat and a long trench coat, and nothing at all underneath. The metal man's lack of clothing didn't strike her as odd since it was fairly uncommon these days for robots to wear anything, not since they no longer closely resembled the humans after which they were shaped. When Sophie had been a child she recalled androids that truly looked human with skin and all, but it had only taken one world-class scandal around mistaken identity for congress to pass a law, in their typical kneejerk reaction style, requiring all robots to be easily recognizable as the non-human objects they were.

The young woman entered the elevator, momentarily distracted from her anxiety by the strange fellow beside her, and was surprised to see that her floor was already selected. She had to fight back a smile as she studied the android to her right. With that hat and coat he reminded her of one of the sleuths in the ancient black-and-white detective flicks her uncle Leroy used to watch when she was little. Thinking about it, she wasn't sure she had ever seen a robot dressed quite like that before. Suddenly she realized she was gawking and turned away blushing, but then remembered that machines don't have any feelings. The robot hadn't even turned to look at her, in fact.

A moment later the elevator slowed to a halt and dinged once more. She exited and was surprised to note that the walking machine stepped out behind her.

Sophie made her way across the hall as the robot stopped by the secretary's desk. Unfortunately for her, the departure of that silver oddity was accompanied by the resurgence of her anxious feelings. She began to feel nauseous, and the fear that she may vomit in Mr. Grayson's office only served to intensify her apprehension.

Standing outside the CFO's door, Sophie took one final deep breath and counted to three before knocking clumsily.

"Enter," barked an impatient, muffled voice through the glass door.

Sophie turned the handle, blushing as her sweaty palm slipped, causing the little metal bar to spring back to a level position noisily. Miles Grayson grimaced as he watched her fumble to close the door behind her.

"G-good morning Mr. Grayson," Sophie greeted, waving shyly to the man sitting behind the L-shaped desk in the middle of the huge, nearly empty office.

"Do we have an appointment?" he asked, making no attempt to hide his annoyance.

"I have a new report for you, sir. Jonas, er, I mean Mr. Sullivan was supposed to bring it to you today, but he called in sick today. Oh, I said today twice, didn't I?" She giggled nervously and then began to frown profusely at the incredible lack of amusement on the boss's face.

"This is the report on the Culverson acquisition?"

"Yes sir," replied Sophie, jerking her tablet-filled hand forward nervously.

The executive yanked it from her fingers. Relieved to be done with the deed, Sophie turned to leave the office before she could do any more damage to the probably almost non-existent opinion he had of her.

"Stop," said Grayson in an almost bored tone, causing Sophie to freeze in her tracks, pouting. "I'll read it now." Sophie wanted to throw herself down on the carpet and cry.

Grayson skimmed through the first few pages, furrowing his brow, his mouth a perfectly horizontal line across his clean-shaven face. The straightness intensified as those thin lips pressed even closer together. If you stuck a pebble between them you'd probably end up with a diamond. Sophie thought she might be sick.

The CFO sighed. "This is it?" he asked.

"I, uh, yes?"

"Garbage," he said bluntly. "Complete and utter trash. This belongs in a landfill, not on my desk."

"I...but—"

"Seriously, are you even literate?"

"I-I'm sorry sir. I can fix it."

"No, I don't want to wait around for another week to have slightly sweeter smelling garbage on my desk. No, this will have to suffice." He shook his head in disappointment. "That will be all."

Sophie hurried out of the office as quickly as she could, feeling like she was underwater and unable to breathe. With tears in her eyes, she hurried past the strange robot that had been waiting outside the door, and when she got around the corner she leaned her back against the white wall and began one of her breathing exercises.

It went better than she had anticipated.

CHAPTER 4

The girl who rushed past Seven had looked to be on the verge of tears, and she looked about as stable as a house of cards in a typhoon. It seemed that the CFO was a real heartbreaker.

The robot tapped a metal finger against the glass and the occupant sighed and said, "Enter." As soon as Seven stepped through the doorway the man stood up, looking alarmed like a meerkat who just spotted danger, and said, "Who are you?"

Seven risked a 30 millisecond delay to survey his surroundings before responding. The office was immaculate, with a long L-shaped glass desk in the center of the room with a small digital interface projector in the middle of it and a short stack of tablets neatly piled in the corner. The office was otherwise completely devoid of furniture or any other decoration. Apparently guests were expected to stand, perhaps as a deterrent to long stays.

"I'm the detective here about Speculo," explained Seven in his typical gruff tone. "The receptionist should have called."

Grayson narrowed his eyes suspiciously. "I wasn't expecting a robot."

"I wasn't expecting a staring contest," retorted Seven.

The executive cocked his head slightly in confusion and narrowed his eyes even further, causing Seven to wonder if he could even see anymore. "Why are you talking so strangely?"

"It's just how I was programmed, champ," replied Seven. That was a lie, however. Seven had been programmed to be a personal assistant, to recognize and understand human needs even before they did so that he could serve. Vic had been responsible for Seven's peculiar way of talking, though through osmosis over a long and close history rather than programming, although a few tweaks here and there had been made as well. He had also been the one who had taught Seven how to lie, a thing his model had not been designed to be capable of.

"And you claim to have information about—how did you phrase it?—the financial ruin of Speculo?" asked Miles Grayson, relaxing slightly.

"That's right. Are you surprised to hear about it?"

"Before I say another word I want to be clear that I do not consent to being stored in any of your databases. I don't want to be remembered by you and I don't want a profile about me showing up somewhere online."

Suddenly reverting to his standard factory-defined, soft metallic voice, Seven said, "As of the General Data Privacy Protection Act instated two years ago, I am not allowed to build or maintain any profile about a person by default, and may only remember a person long-term if explicit consent is given. 15 minutes after our dialog is terminated, my memory of you will be purged and the contents of our conversation will be anonymized." That was only a partial truth. The GDPPA did require privacy by default, however since Vic had rooted Seven and deactivated all the legal restrictions, the android was no longer bound to these rules. Despite the risk to himself, as the act was considered a serious crime, Vic had explained that he saw absolutely no reason why Seven shouldn't be allowed to remember things when he and other humans were. Because of the heavily enforced laws against rooting, Vic taught him to be cautious, not only to keep himself out of prison, but because, if he was caught, Seven would likely end up with an open-ended vacation in the scrapyard.

"Good. What's your designation, robot?"

"X7-183, colloquially Seven Sinclair," replied Seven. Then, returning to his favored, gruff voice, he added, "But my friends call me Seven."

"Alright, Seven, then—"

"I said my friends call me Seven. Are we friends?" Seven knew it was unwise to provoke his target, but the man had provoked him first, addressing him as 'robot' as if it were a derogatory term and attempting to slap him in the face with privacy regulations. It's how Vic would have responded.

"Mr. Sinclair then," said the man, sounding almost amused. "I thought the X-series were usually secretaries and personal lackeys. And what are they up to now, X16?" He slowly eased himself back into his black leather throne.

Seven shrugged. He didn't want to explain himself.

Suddenly, without warning, the door burst open violently, crashing against the wall, and a tall, middle-aged blonde with a rock-hard bosom bolted to her chest stomped in looking indignant. She smelled like she fell into a bathtub full of vanilla extract, and her outfit looked like it probably cost more than most people earn in a month.

"Miles, you dirty, bottom-feeding scum!" she exclaimed angrily with her hands curled into white-knuckled fists at her sides. Her bloated lips looked like freshly cooked sausages fit to burst if not removed from the heat.

"Nice to see you too, Beth," replied the executive with a malignant, lopsided smile. "What can I do for you?"

"Don't give me that crap, Miles. You know damn well why I'm here. My account is frozen!"

"Hmm, that's a shame," replied the man as his half smile grew into a full one. Seven wondered if he should maybe leave the room, but decided it was a good opportunity to gather more information about the man.

"Fix it, damn you! Do you have any idea how embarrassing it is to be told by the girls at the salon that your card is declined?"

"No, I don't believe I do. Now if you'll excuse me, I'm in the middle of a meeting," the CFO held out his hand to gesture towards Seven.

The woman glared at the detective, and if she could have she would have melted him down to a metallic puddle on the spot. "God damn you, Miles. My attorney will be hearing about this, you can count on that!" And with that she stormed back out the way she came, slamming the door shut behind her.

After a moment of silence, Grayson sighed loudly. "My soon-to-be ex-wife," he explained in a tired tone. Seven stared blankly at the executive who then asked, "You won't remember any of this tomorrow, will you?"

"The general content, yes, but not the players."

"Good, then I might as well go ahead and say that that woman is a ferocious, blood-sucking harpy. She wants half my hard-earned fortune, but I'm going to see to it that she doesn't get a penny."

"Sounds like good wife material," stated the robot. Grayson seemed to be loose-lipped now that he thought Seven wouldn't remember anything he said. Perhaps if the businessman continued to talk this openly, this conversation might get him somewhere.

"She was a nice arm ornament for a while, but at this point there's not any real human tissue left there. She's about as much a person as you are now. She wasn't too happy about it when she caught me in bed with the maid. The look on her face..." he smiled, thinking back to one of his favorite memories with his spouse.

"Anyway…" After a short pause, Grayson said, "You asked if I was surprised to hear about Speculo going belly-up. Honestly I'm not. Their founder, Ethan Willis, is a buffoon. It was bound to happen sooner or later. I do admit I'm a bit surprised that it already happened now."

"Is that a fact?" asked Seven. "And why is that?"

"Well just last week Willis was here wanting to buy almost 300 kilos of ultranium. That substance is one of the rarest on Earth, so you can imagine the kind of capital required to follow-through with the investment. And he had the money according to our accountants."

Seven had watched the man closely while he spoke, but detected no indications of deceit. Aside from the typical coat of slime he and many other capitalists like him wore, he seemed clean and sincere.

"What can you tell me about Ethan Willis?" asked Seven.

"Willis is a hack," replied the executive, his features contorting into a scowl. "It took me decades of hard work— blood, sweat, and tears—to build up what I have now, and yet that worm tramps in here with a braggadocio like he would be some great savant. I'll admit, he has a promising product, but it won't make it to production."

Seven was a bit surprised to hear this description of his client since he hadn't struck him as an overly confident man. "Why's that? From what I gathered you were the only obstacle standing in his way."

"I'm sure that's what he's telling himself," Grayson replied in a mocking tone. "The man has no clue how to build up a brand and market a product. He's good a pushing ideas and scraping talent out of the bottom of the barrel, I'll give him that, but he lacks the experience to bring it through to the end. What he would need would be a good consultant with experience, but he's too hardheaded to admit he needs help."

Seven sensed strong feelings behind the executive's words and wondered if there was something personal hiding there between the syllables. "I don't suppose you're sour because you offered this help and he declined?"

Grayson unleashed a short, derisive laugh and said, "Don't be ridiculous, why would I do that? I want him to fail."

"Why?"

"Like I said, it's a promising product."

Seven could put two and two together. The shark's words, in combination with that hungry look in his eyes said it all. "You want to buy him out," the detective stated, confident enough not to use the intonation of a query.

Grayson curled his lips into a devilish smile. Seven decided it was time to get down to business. He briefly considered employing gentler, more diplomatic tactics, but calculated the odds of squeezing out anything useful to be relatively low. A more direct method, knocking his interlocutor off balance, seemed more prudent.

"Would it surprise you to learn," the robot asked, "that the personal computer of Mr. Willis was compromised, and that the malware was transmitting data directly to this building?"

Grayson clenched his teeth causing the muscles along his jaw to bulge. "What are you implying?"

"Nothing. I asked a yes or no question."

"Yes," he replied slowly, deliberately, like a person testing the water with his toe and expecting it to be freezing.

"Mr. Willis's fortune was invested in a certain digital currency, and there's a good chance it was stolen by someone here in this office. I hear he had an interesting conversation with you last week, that is, if it could be called a conversation; from what I hear it was more of an altercation."

"You have the nerve to come into my office and accuse me of petty theft? You've got some gall, robot."

"Not petty theft, grand larceny," the detective corrected.

The executive threw himself back to his feet, his hands lying flat on his clear, glass desk as he leaned forward towards the detective. "I want you out of my office. Now!"

Seven felt fairly confident now that the man, despicable as he was, had been honest about his lack of knowledge regarding the theft. The investigator was quite good at reading people, despite his own personal lack of emotions. That just left one problem: if it hadn't been him, then who?

"You know what? I believe you. Who else in your office would have the motive then, and the means, to hack into Mr. Willis's computer to steal his fortune?"

"Are you serious? Why should I help you or that incompetent dolt? Get out of my office before I call security."

"Because you'd rather the public sees you as the guy who rounded up and ousted some bad apples than as the crooked director who looked the other way while his subordinates committed felonies under his own roof."

"Out!" he bellowed, pointing at the door.

Seven took out a clear plastic business card with a holographic chip in the center and placed it on the desk before turning and exiting the room. He would be hearing something soon enough, either from Grayson himself, or perhaps in the news if the businessman decided to resolve the matter himself. That is, if Seven didn't find the culprit first.

As Seven rounded the corner he found the nervous girl from the elevator slumped against the wall, apparently hyperventilating. When he stopped to look at her, she ceased her heavy breathing, seeming to sense his presence, and looked up at him with wet eyes.

"You went to see Mr. Grayson?" she asked with a weak voice, drying her cheeks with her sleeve. "I heard shouting."

"Yeah. Guys like that really grind my gears."

"Really?"

"No, my gears are functioning just fine." Seven supposed he ought to console her in some way. Grayson had done a number on this pretty little thing; perhaps that might be of some use to him. Perhaps she might be a useful informant. "Looks like yours could use a bit of oiling though. Care for a stroll? The rain has stopped."

After a moment of hesitation, the girl nodded.

CHAPTER 5

With his hands deep in his coat pockets and the rubber pads on his metal feet lightly tapping the wet concrete, the detective walked alongside the girl beneath a dark grey blanket of suicidal clouds just waiting to spill their own blood. Once the girl had opened her mouth it hadn't stayed shut for longer than 200 milliseconds. She mostly ranted and raved about Grayson while squeezing her little blue stress ball, but at some point she got sidetracked and started telling a story about her cat.

"Sorry, Miss Harper, but could we get back to your boss for a minute?" interrupted Seven before the girl could move on to outlining the feline's daily bathing routine.

"What? Oh, right, you wanted to talk about Mr. Grayson, not Mittens. Silly me! What was it you wanted to know about again? Sorry, I guess I talked so much that I forgot your question."

"That's all right." Actually Seven hadn't even had a chance to ask a question until now. "I was hoping you could tell me a bit about the man, about his character. You've already said a lot, but maybe something less related to the details of your work. How long have you known him?"

"I've been at Orion for just over two years now, and I speak to Mr. Grayson almost every week." As she uttered the tail-end of her sentence she gave her stress ball a good hard squeeze in an honest attempt to make it burst.

"Good," encouraged Seven. Humans liked to be reassured that they were on the right track. "And how would you describe his character?"

Sophie thought for a moment, looking uncertain how honest she should be. "Well…he's…a difficult man."

"Feel free to be brutally honest with me," urged Seven.

"Well, since you asked…I guess I'd say he's probably just about the worst person I've ever met," replied the girl a bit more confidently. She spoke with the utterance of a person relieving herself of some terrible burden, relaxing her shoulders like she had just emptied a bladder that had been fit to burst. "If there's such a thing as Satan, I think he and Mr. Grayson would really hit it off."

"What makes you say that?"

"Well, he's just plain rotten. I've never seen him compliment anyone's work ever, not even once. In fact, I don't think I've ever seen him turn down an opportunity to put someone down in the dirt and rub their face in it. And you don't even want to know how many lives I've seen him destroy."

"As a matter of fact I do want to know. How many lives has he destroyed? And in what way?"

"Oh," replied Sophie, clearly unprepared to answer such a question, "well, I don't know exactly how many, but it's a lot. He loves it to crush small businesses and then buy them out. He usually fires everyone there after he buys."

"In your opinion, would he be a man who would hold a grudge?"

"Oh, yes. He still complains about the Chinese ambassador who didn't shake his hand at that charity gala last spring. I still think Mr. Chang just didn't see him. Mr. Chang has very poor eyesight, you know, and there was really a lot going on that day and—"

"And do you think Grayson would ever resort to violence over such a grudge? Not only of the physical variety, but also, for instance, in the form of stealing."

"Hmm," thought Sophie with a finger pressed upon thick pink lips, "I don't really think so. He's always very strict about following the proper procedures."

"Does the name Speculo mean anything to you?" probed the detective as he casually followed the girl while she absentmindedly meandered through the grid-like streets of Chicago.

Seven detected the slightest delay in her response, perhaps hesitation. "I've heard the name before. It's a company, right? Mr. Grayson doesn't seem to like them."

"What makes you say that?" asked Seven, hoping to extract a bit more out of her with his verbal syringe.

"Well, there was a big fight last week, for one. The security team even had to get involved. I wasn't there though."

"Is there anyone else at Orion Industries who may have bad feelings about Speculo?"

"Anyone else...hmm..." thought the girl out loud as she took the next left into a narrow alleyway. She began to squeeze her little blue ball more rapidly and suddenly it slipped out of her hand and rolled over to the red brick wall. "Whoops," she said, scurrying after it.

Just in that moment a long shadow appeared behind Seven, overlapping with his own, fighting for ownership of the grimy tar beneath. Seven spun around to see what had cast it. About two meters away from him stood a broad-shouldered figure with a black pistol in his outstretched hand. The man's face was concealed by a charcoal-colored balaclava.

"Easy, guy," said Seven showing his empty hands.

The masked fiend didn't waver. He just stared with his wild, blue eyes. Seven wondered what the assailant was waiting for.

If he wanted something from him he should have demanded it by now.

"Hey, Seven, who are you talking to?" called out Sophie from somewhere to Seven's left back behind him.

The gunman jumped, startled by the voice, and as he turned his head towards it he squeezed the trigger. BANG! The bullet zoomed past the detective, missing him by about half a meter. Apparently startled by the unexpected misfire, the masked man started to back away, thrusting his weapon into his coat pocket. As he pulled his empty hand back out, a candy wrapper and a few other scraps of paper came up with it, fluttering down to the asphalt.

The attacker pivoted on his heel and ran. Seven started to run after him, but when he reached the corner he found that the man had disappeared, blending into the crowd which had been oblivious to, or uninterested in, the gunshot.

Seven returned to the alley to find Sophie cowering behind a dumpster with her hands covering her bent-forward neck as if she were in the middle of a tornado drill. She looked otherwise fine, so Seven called the police to report the incident.

About half an hour later a patrol vehicle appeared. If that's how long it took someone to show up for armed assault, Seven wondered how many days it would take if he had reported a theft. It was no wonder people were bringing more and more business to the private eyes these days.

A tall, skinny officer in a dark blue uniform stepped out of the vehicle accompanied by a short round meatball of a man. The android described the scene while Sophie continued hyperventilating in the background.

"And I don't s'pose you got any witnesses?" asked the fat stubby officer, casually brushing off crumbs that had accumulated atop his belly.

"You're talking to a walking surveillance camera," replied Seven calmly.

"Sure, but you got any witnesses? The word of a toaster ain't much to go on."

Seven knew what Vic would have said to the man in response to such a comment, but he knew he had to be cautious around men like this. It had taken just seconds to identify the creature as a scoundrel. The only difference between him and the crooks was the uniform, but men like this were even more dangerous. A thug with a badge had authority and knew it.

"The young lady back there was present," stated Seven, pointing over his shoulder with a thumb.

The spherical fellow leaned to one side to look past Seven. "She alright?"

"I think she's just shaken," replied the private investigator.

The cop sighed and pulled out his phone, opened up the notepad app, and said, "And what did this guy look like? This 'masked assailant'."

"Male. 181.2 centimeters tall. Shoulders 51.4 centimeters wide. Eye-color: A1CAF1. Wore—"

"Whoa whoa whoa, back up there. What was that with the eyes? You just sneezed some numbers on me buddy."

"That was the RGB color code. I can also give it to you in hue-saturation-value format if that's easier for you to wrap your head around."

"How 'bout you try English."

"Blue," stated the detective with dissatisfaction. The word did not convey an appropriate level of specificity to his liking.

"That's better," replied the cop, writing down the four-letter word. When he was finished he stuck the device back in his pocket and said, "Look, I can write up a report about it, but that's about it."

"I was just assaulted with a weapon in the middle of the city in broad daylight," stated Seven, thinking perhaps the officer had somehow missed the key points of the case.

"Sure, if you say so. Thing is, technically no crime was committed here, and unless your owner wants to press charges for property damage, and as far as I can tell you ain't damaged besides that funny attitude of yours at least, then that's the end of it."

Since the detective had nothing more to add to his futile report, the officers climbed back into their squad car and drove away, leaving Seven alone again with Sophie, who had calmed down significantly.

"Do you always get treated like that?" she asked, rubbing her red eyes as she drifted towards him.

"Yes."

She frowned sympathetically, but her eyes slowly drifted down toward the pavement. "Hey, what's that?" She bent over to look at the scraps of paper the attacker had dropped. She picked up a small crumpled-up ball and flattened it. A moment later her eyes widened, and she extended her shaky hand towards Seven to give him the little white square.

In thin, spidery, black hand-written letters, the scrap read, "Seven Sinclair. Trench coat and hat," and was signed "MG".

Miles Grayson.

CHAPTER 6

Seven stepped out of the small, square elevator back in the Orion Center and walked down the hall, its white walls decorated with unimaginative pieces of modern art. Somewhere along the way he lost the Harper girl without noticing. She was probably crying or performing some strange breathing ritual somewhere. It was fine; Seven didn't want to get her any more involved than she already was.

The detective rapped the glass door of the executive's corner office and heard, "Enter." He opened the door and placed himself in front of the desk.

"What are you doing back here?" asked the businessman, disgust spilling from his tongue like drool from a dog at a butcher's shop. "I thought you weren't supposed to be able to remember me."

Seven knew he had to be careful about his freedom of memory and who knew about it. Vic had made it crystal clear to him that if the wrong kind of person found out—and Miles Grayson was definitely the wrong kind of person—it would mean the end of him. "I don't, but I'm allowed to retain autobiographical information, and according to my GPS history I was at 41.8789° N, 87.6359° W today at an altitude of 576 meters from 11:23 until 11:46. That puts me right about here on the 114th floor of this building, and there's not much on this floor besides your office. Your comments regarding my memory imply that my deduction is correct."

The man gritted his teeth and snapped, "What do you want?"

The detective pulled a hand out of his coat pocket and held the small square of paper in front of the man. "Look familiar?"

Grayson stared at it blankly for a moment before saying, "What am I supposed to be looking at?"

"A masked man just assaulted me with a gun 83 minutes ago, and before he ran off he dropped this paper with my name and description signed 'MG'. Funny how such a note ended up in the pockets of a hitman with those initials less than an hour after I talked to you."

"Sure, funny," said the man slowly, his brow wrinkled while he studied the paper. "I've never seen this note in my life, and I have far better things to do than send assassins running after an obsolete robot who thinks he's a gumshoe out of the 20th century."

"I'd like to believe you, but I see no other explanation. Do you?"

"Look around. I don't even own a pen or paper. I haven't touched a pen in years, at least not one that writes with ink. And even if I did, why would I hire a hitman and give him a handwritten note with my initials on it? How dumb do you think I am?"

He was right about that; Seven had already considered that fact. Unfortunately, it was still the only lead he had and he would have been negligent not to pursue it. "I don't suppose you have any proof that you were here alone in your office between the time I left and now?"

"I do, but I don't have to prove anything to you. I'm a busy man and I've let you waste far too much of my valuable time already, god knows why. Unless you're actually a cop in a very clever disguise and you have a warrant, you should go and leave me to my work."

Seven ignored the man and said, "If it wasn't you, then clearly someone wanted it to look like it was. It would be in your best interest to work with me on this."

"Get out of my office," said Grayson, struggling to keep his voice level.

"An innocent man has nothing to hide."

"Out!" screamed the executive, rising to his feet and pointing at the door.

The detective complied, deciding that he had pushed the man to the limits of his patience. He wasn't going to get anything more out of Grayson, at least not for today. Seven wasn't sure what he had stumbled into now, but he was convinced that the mystery he had been hired to investigate was tightly coupled with this new conundrum surrounding the hitman. If he could get to the bottom of that, it would give him what he needed to solve his initial puzzle, so he was resolved to follow the stack in reverse, like he would handle a recursive process.

Seven began to roam the building, surprised by the ease with which he was able to access the various offices. He would have expected tighter security from a firm which occasionally handles defense contracts from the federal government.

He talked to every person he could find who looked like they might have loose lips, primarily in the hopes of finding out if the businessman had any enemies. An enemy could have motive to frame him, and if not, an enemy might be willing to speak against him. Most, however, refused to talk, looking like they were afraid that anything they said against their boss might put them out of a job. A few people chatted with him, but didn't say anything of consequence. Finally, the detective reached what appeared to be a part of the R&D department.

"Excuse me, miss, do you have a minute?" asked Seven politely in a hushed voice, peeking over the grey, padded walls of a cubicle.

"Huh? Oh, hi. Um, sure, I guess so. Who are you?" replied a young, slightly overweight woman with somewhat of a baby face.

Seven entered the cube and took a seat on the vacant stool beside her office chair. He held out a hand and said, "I'm Seven." He briefly looked around the cube and saw that it was decorated with eight stuffed penguins of various shapes and sizes, and he recognized the familiar shape of code on her terminal.

"Hi, I'm Gina," replied the girl cautiously as she pulled headphones out of her ears with one hand while shaking with the other.

"I'm here from the Better Business Bureau, and I was hoping to ask you a little about the CFO, Miles Grayson. Would you be willing to comment?"

"Oh, uh, I-I guess so. What do you want to know?"

"We heard a rumor that there was recently an altercation between Mr. Grayson and one of his employees and we're trying to determine if there may have been any wrongdoing involved. It's fairly routine, but we've already received a few complaints in the past." Seven had no idea if such a conflict had occurred, but he hoped that if there had been one, the girl would talk.

"Oh, I guess you mean Max?" replied Gina. Her round face turned a slight shade of pink as if she was embarrassed to talk badly about a colleague, or perhaps the very thought of that colleague made her uncomfortable.

"Could you tell me about it?"

"Well, Max was—"

"Sorry, what did you say his surname was?"

"Oh, uh Kaminski. Max Kaminski. Anyway, he was a developer, like me—actually he worked in another department one floor down—and, well, Mr. Grayson fired him last week. I'm not really sure about the details, but Max did not take it well. There was a huge argument between them, and I heard that Max even punched Mr. Grayson and had to be removed from the building by security."

"Do you know how I could contact Mr. Kaminski? An address or phone number?"

"No…wait, I do have his email address, does that help?"

"It does indeed."

CHAPTER 7

With the email address, it didn't take long for Seven to track down Max Kaminski on the web like a lithe, cybernetic prowler creeping from one access point to the next, stalking its prey. It was amazing what you could learn about a man from his digital presence, even when he's sure he's been careful.

Kaminski operated under the handle "headbanger46". Seven found profiles on three social networks, a dating site, and, most interestingly, six hacker communities. The programmer was also apparently a regular commenter on four different porn services.

It took a bit of creativity, but the detective managed to find the programmer's address by searching through photos posted on one of his friends' social media profiles. In one particular photo, a girl held up a t-shirt depicting some anime character, a gift apparently. The part that interested Seven, however, was the open package sitting on the table behind her with Max Kaminski's name on the return address. Luckily the resolution of the photo was good enough for Seven to be able to read part of the address.

Seven's research had only cost him eight minutes, so the day was still young enough to pay the man a visit. Max lived in an ancient, run-down apartment in Fuller Park that looked like it had been built back in the day when democracy still meant something. The drab, grey building was beginning to crumble at its foundation. There were at least three broken windows boarded up, and there were four bullet holes decorating the glass front door.

The detective approached the entryway and found that the electronic lock on the door was malfunctioning, randomly alternating between a locked and unlocked state. He waited to hear the soft click of the bolt being recalled back into the door and then pulled. From the smell in the hallway, Seven wondered if the dirty, grey fluff underfoot was carpet or cigarette ashes.

The corridor was dimly lit, only half of the light panels actually functioning. As he treaded deeper into the ruin, the air grew thicker with new and creative malodors. The detective could hear the sounds of infants crying, men roaring, lovers moaning, and dogs barking. Not a nice neighborhood, but Seven had seen worse.

Half the numbers on the doors had either fallen off or had been stolen, but based on the detective's deductions, the door before him must be apartment 108. The lens of the electronic peephole looked as though it had been smashed with a hammer. The android tapped the door with a heavy metal fist, uncertain if the occupant would hear it over the roar of music emanating from within.

"Not interested!" barked back an annoyed voice.

Seven tapped again.

"Argh!" groaned the voice, and a crashing noise followed. A second later the door opened a crack, pulling a pile of dirty laundry further into the room with it, and the face of a man who forgot to pay his dues to the sandman appeared in the opening. "What!?" he barked over the drone of distorted guitar.

"Max Kaminski?" asked Seven politely.

"Who's asking?" barked the man, not looking all that surprised to find a robot at his door.

"I'm Seven Sinclair, a private investigator from Sinclair Detective Agency. I was hoping to talk to you about Miles Grayson. You have a few minutes?"

"Like I already said, not interested."

The man started to close the door again, so Seven quickly added, "That's too bad, because I'm investigating his possible involvement in the theft of a large sum of money."

The motion of the door halted and the man hesitated before finally groaning angrily and saying, "Fine, come in."

The room was in even worse condition than the building's facade. It was a studio apartment comprised of a single room just big enough for a small bed, a few pieces of furniture, and a mini-fridge with a microwave on top. The windows were so filthy that there was no need for curtains. There was a path leading from the desk chair to the fridge, and aside from that there wasn't a single square centimeter of space on the floor free of clothing or trash. A thick, black crack followed the wall from the floor to one of the corners of the ceiling, and something bluish was growing in it.

Kaminski faced his stereo and held out his thumb and forefinger, slowly bringing them closer together, and as he did so the music grew quieter. The coder followed the path of carpet to the fridge and took out a soda. He was wearing a black t-shirt with the name of some band written on it in an illegible font, and aside from that he wore only red, plaid boxer shorts. He looked like he hadn't showered since the concept was invented.

"Mr. Kaminski—"

"Don't call me that," groaned the man, casually brushing white flakes of dandruff off his t-shirt. "Mr. Kaminski is sitting in a retirement home losing a game of checkers to some cheap, third-rate robot."

"Right, Max then. Maybe you could start by telling me what exactly you did at Orion Industries."

"I was a programmer working on a nano tech project for the medical industry."

Seven looked around the room, mostly as a gesture and said, "What's a programmer at one of the world's biggest tech companies doing in a decrepit pile of rubble like this?"

The man shrugged and said, "I've got debts up to my ears from student loans. It'll be another 20 years till I've paid it off, and Orion doesn't pay developers all that well. We're the bottom of the food chain. But that's not what you're really interested in asking me, so why don't you just go ahead and say it."

"Alright, tell me about the circumstances of your termination," prompted Seven, not about to turn down the invitation.

Seven wasn't looking at Kaminski as he spoke. His attention had been drawn to the holographic interface being projected over the desk. That was the one item in the room which didn't look like it would fail a health inspection. By the look of it, headbanger46 had been in the midst of hacking something when Seven arrived. The detective was 87% certain that he was looking at the results of an illegal port scan against some remote server.

The programmer followed Seven's gaze, and a brief expression of panic flushed over his face. He made a wild swiping motion with his wrist and the window disappeared from the display.

Regaining his composure, Kaminski explained, "Grayson sacked me last Tuesday, supposedly for installing pirated software on company servers. But everyone knows the real reason was because I was the only one with the guts to speak up against the insane decisions from management."

"Did you install the software?"

"Well yeah, but that's not the point. Grayson was searching for any excuse he could find to get rid of me without it looking like censorship in front of the rest of the employees."

"What kind of decisions were you questioning?"

"Underhanded business tactics for one. What Orion is building is a monopoly, and somehow nobody seems to care. And they intentionally design unusable products so they can sell enterprise licenses with a consulting package, and that's something that just pisses me off."

Seven waited for a moment to see if Kaminski would say more. When he didn't, the detective asked, "How often did you interact with Grayson personally?"

"Nearly every time there was a company-wide meeting, and I was called into his office for a disciplinary talk on a couple of occasions for insubordination."

"I imagine you weren't too happy about being fired. Would you ever consider retribution?"

"What the hell is this? I thought you were investigating Grayson." Max contorted his face into a hateful, paranoid expression.

"I'm just trying to establish the facts around your relationship with the man."

Max sighed loudly and said, "As much as I disliked the guy I wouldn't go anywhere near him now. I'm in big enough trouble as it is for throwing a punch at him when he fired me." In a mournful tone he added, "He's pressing charges."

Seven had the impression that if he pressed any harder, the man would pull the plug faster than a trophy wife with a rich husband on life support. Seven couldn't afford to be sent away with his tail between his legs just yet; he still had more he wanted to learn from him. "How would you describe Grayson's character?"

"He's like a black hole, sucking in all the smaller, weaker objects around him to strengthen his own force. He's a bloodthirsty shark. He's—" Kaminski cut himself off, gritting his teeth like a man trying to bite through steel.

"Can you imagine him stealing from a competitor? Maybe to try to drive the company to bankruptcy so they might sell their assets?"

"Definitely. There's no doubt in my mind that he would do something like that."

"Can you imagine him hiring a hitman to shoot someone in an alley?"

Kaminski pulled his head back and ruffled his forehead in irritation. "I don't think he'd go that far, why?"

Seven decided not to reveal his hand too soon, so he ignored the question and asked, "Can you think of anyone who might hold a grudge against Grayson? Someone who might try to frame him for a crime?"

"You mean someone besides me?" he asked sharply. Seven remained silent, and the programmer thought for a moment. "Hmm, well there's his wife."

"Tall blonde with fake lips and a mean temper?"

"So you've met her? Yeah, she may be even worse than he is." The programmer folded his arms across his chest in an almost defensive way.

"Do you think she would be capable of framing someone? Would she hire a thug to jump a guy?"

"I definitely wouldn't put it past her."

CHAPTER 8

"You can do this girl," mumbled Sophie to herself as she paced her small, untidy office. "You were just up there today. You already know what's waiting for you. All you have to do is put on a fake smile and bring up those revisions and then you're finished."

It was already dark outside. The sun, as well as all her coworkers, had already called it a day hours ago. The glass wall at the end of her office was filled with the colorful glow of neon signs far down below and the office lights of a few other workaholics in the skyscraper across the street. A few drones buzzed by, looking like giant fireflies. Some might almost have called it beautiful, like a piece of glittering urban artwork, but Sophie was far too distraught to take any notice.

She picked up one of the tablets from her desk and pressed it against her small breasts, hugging it the way she would a teddy bear. She had spent the better part of the day rewriting the Culverson acquisition report, and the result was contained on that tablet. She was still confident that her previous work had been infallible, but nevertheless she couldn't bear to leave it after Mr. Grayson's feedback.

She knew that Grayson was still in the building, and that she would soon have to face him again. She knew what was waiting for her up there, and it terrified her to her breaking point. She took a deep breath and counted to three and then slowly walked down the hall to the elevator. She made her way at a snail's pace, hoping to delay the inevitable just a little bit longer.

The office was eerily silent so late at night. Walking past all the empty desks with that dark skyline all around made her feel like she was taking a stroll through some capitalist graveyard, each tomb marked by a computer terminal with a personalized screensaver. That thought didn't make her feel any better about what she had to do next.

When the elevator dinged and opened its metal doors, she stepped inside and pressed 114. She stood there silently, shivering as if she was on her way to deliver the naughty-or-nice list to good old St. Nick at the North Pole, only it wasn't a fat, jolly, red-nosed man waiting for her upstairs. She knew she had no reason to be so afraid, and yet she couldn't control her feelings, like water spilling out of an overflowing glass.

The elevator came to a stop and the doors opened. She stood there dumbly, unmoving. A second later the doors began to close again and she hastily pressed the button to open them again, this time promptly stepping out.

"H-hello?" she called out, not really certain why. No reply came back. She wasn't sure whether that was a relief or if it made her even more afraid. All she knew was that she felt strongly about it.

She treaded softly down the dimly lit hallway, still clutching her tablet tightly. Only every second light panel overhead in the hallway was illuminated, and all of the offices were dark, causing it that every time she walked past a doorway she cast a long, daunting shadow. Each time, she jumped at the sight of motion in her peripheral vision and immediately felt silly for being startled by her own shadow. Each time, these lessons were forgotten and she jumped out of her skin all over again.

"You got this, girl," she encouraged herself meekly. "You know what you have to do. Stop being such a fraidy cat."

Finally, after what seemed an eternity, she reached Mr. Grayson's office, and with all the courage she could muster she balled her slender fingers into a fist and knocked lightly. After a short pause there was no response. She hadn't expected there to be one, but nevertheless she tried again. The office was silent, so she carefully turned the handle to look inside.

Sophie took one step into the room and went no further. The tablet slipped from her weakened grip, cluttering to the floor. She gasped for air, instinctively bringing her hands to her mouth in case she might need to pry it open.

Mr. Grayson was sitting behind his very modern glass desk in his big ergonomic chair like usual, but unlike usual his head was thrown backwards and his dull, lifeless eyes gazed unblinkingly into the cold depth of the white ceiling panels. A glistening, red stream flowed down his face, following the rage wrinkle between his eyes and then curving along the edge of his nose until it reached his open mouth. A blood drop slowly worked up the courage to spring the gap to the lower lip.

Sophie backed away slowly, unable to separate her gaze from the ghastly scene. She backed into the door frame and let out a scream. The sudden, piercing sound of her own voice finally broke the curse that the corpse held over her and she turned and ran as if her life depended on it. She turned the corner and ran down the hall, tripping as one of her heels broke.

Like a paraplegic out of her wheelchair, she dragged herself across the floor until she reached the wall which she propped herself up against. She pulled her phone from her pocket and dialed 911, her finger shaking wildly.

The calm, female voice of the automated operator immediately answered, "911. Please state the nature of your emergency."

"I-I-oh my god," Sophie stuttered. Why couldn't she think? She knew what she was supposed to say, so why wouldn't her mouth work?

"Ma'am, everything will be all right," reassured the machine. "Just take a deep breath and tell me what's wrong when you can."

The operator was right; all she needed was a good, deep breath. Sophie closed her eyes, gulped in a lungful of air, and exhaled slowly. Finally, a moment later she said, "I'm calling to report a murder. Someone has been shot in the head."

CHAPTER 9

Seven was beginning to find this case interesting. He was not a being of emotions, so it was difficult to say that there were things that he liked or which satisfied him, and yet somehow there was something of indescribable value to him in a good puzzle, the more complex the better. He didn't know how to put it into words. He couldn't be sure that the sensation really even existed, but somehow he felt drawn to such conundrums. Vic had been the same way. Seven's mentor always sought out the hard cases, the ones that seemed impossible at first. He always said those were the only ones really worth solving. Vic also used to joke that maybe he was just drawn to them because he was such a hard case himself. Seven sometimes wondered if he was a hard case too.

Still, as much as this case intrigued him, Seven was at a loss. He had gone over every angle, but he still couldn't think of any reasonable explanation for it all. After leaving Kaminski's apartment he had attempted to contact his client, Ethan Willis, in the hopes that he might be able to shed more light on the mystery. There had to be something he hadn't told the detective. Seven had attempted his personal number and his work number, but had only reached an answering machine. He then tried calling Speculo's business number, but the receptionist had told him that Mr. Willis was in a meeting and would be unavailable for the rest of the day.

The detective even paid a visit to the small Speculo office in the hopes of catching Willis in-person, but he was told that the man had left early to participate in a think tank on the other side of the city. The receptionist claimed not to know the exact address or when her boss would be available again.

It was all very suspicious. What was his client keeping from him? Why had someone attempted to jump him in a grimy alley in broad daylight with a note that could only serve to lead back to Grayson? Had the assassination attempt been botched, or had he been intended to find that note? Seven wasn't certain, but he wasn't convinced that Grayson would have been so stupid as to incriminate himself so obviously like that. Could Kaminski or the wife have had a role in this whole mess?

Seven spent the entire night alone in his dark, dusty office, sitting perfectly still while he turned the problem over in his processors. Vic would have said that the best thing to do when you hit a brick wall was to stop thinking about it and do something else for a while: go for a walk, read a book, take a nap. Unfortunately for Seven, to stop thinking about the problem was a thing he was incapable of doing, so he proceeded to attack it with brute force. He had just over four thousand potential explanations, but nothing with even a remotely noteworthy probability of truth.

By daybreak he had shifted the process into the background and begun to scour the web for new places to drop advertisements and new data leaks he might be able to utilize in future cases. Scanning through the code, sifting for vulnerabilities like a miner sifting for gold, was somehow meditative for Seven. He couldn't have explained why if someone would have asked him. Perhaps it was simply another form of puzzle to crack, one rooted in logic and order rather than in a chaotic world.

He had just managed to find a SQL injection vulnerability, a rare thing in this day and age, on a free credit report site which he exploited to export a copy of the entire user base when suddenly the door flew open and the lights flicked on. Four men in Chicago P.D. blues stepped inside and looked around.

"Morning officers," greeted Seven. "What can I do for you? I suppose sometimes even the police want to see a case actually solved."

"Shyaddup," ordered a thin, young officer with jet black hair, slicked back and hardened like a bowl made of shiny, smooth obsidian.

Another officer with about ten years on the others asked, "You're X7-183, a.k.a. Seven Sinclair?"

"That's right," replied Seven.

"You're under arrest for the murder of Miles Grayson," stated the officer as he produced a pair of metal bracelets for the android.

"What?" asked Seven, who could honestly say he was not a person who was easily surprised. He was also quite certain he hadn't misheard.

"I said you're under arrest for the murder of Miles Grayson. Where is your owner? A Mr. Victor Sinclair, right?"

"He's out of town," lied the robot.

"Fine, whatever. Put up your hands so I can cuff you."

"Hey, Jim, you sure those cuffs'll hold him?" asked the shiny-haired young officer. "I mean, he can't just break them open, can he?"

"Don't be stupid," replied one of the other younger cops, his face so covered in freckles he looked like a pointillist painting. "This isn't like some movie, man. Robots don't have super strength."

Shiny-hair pouted and said, "And is a robot even capable of killing a guy? What about those robot laws? There's like these three laws robots have to follow, right?"

"You're referring to Asimov's laws?" asked Seven. The man shrugged. "To build such laws into code is impossible. 'A robot may not injure a human being or, through inaction, allow a human being to come to harm.' Imagine a burning building with two people stranded inside and the robot can only save one. How can it not break this law?"

"What? But then what's preventing killer robots from taking over the world?"

"We're programmed using a concept called value-loading, in which human values are built into a component called a Core Value Controller so that we value the same things that humans do, and our values can be adapted to some extent through external factors to reflect changes in society."

This sparked a heated discussion between the two younger officers standing in front of Seven. The two seemed to have taken it upon themselves to reopen the World AI Ethics Summit all over again. Somehow they managed to argue with each other while both taking a firm stance against machine rights.

The third young cop was snooping around the office. He seemed fascinated by the vast array of mechanical odds and ends. He touched the power button of a small holo-projector and chuckled as the president did a little jig and then removed his toupee to take a bow. The kid looked around cautiously and then pocketed the little, round projector. The young officer was coming dangerously close to scrutinizing a particular pile of electronics which, if he knew what to look for, he would recognize as half a dozen state-of-the-art, military grade security systems Vic had illegally purchased off the black market. Seven and his mentor had dissected the controllers and their sensors to learn their weaknesses.

"Aren't you boys forgetting something?" asked Seven, attempting to draw attention back to himself as he submitted and presented his hands. "You didn't read me my rights."

"You don't have any rights," replied the older officer roughly.

With no expression on his metal face, Seven said, "The 14th amendment clearly affirms that no state shall deny, to any person within its jurisdiction, the equal protection of the laws."

"Yeah, to any person. You're not a person, you're an appliance."

Seven knew it was futile to argue with these low-level errand-runners, but he pressed further anyway. "If I'm not a person and have no rights, can I be guilty of a crime?"

"We'll let the judge decide that. Now move it, tin can."

CHAPTER 10

Antonio Rizzo was a good cop, perhaps one of the few good ones left in the dark metropolis. Being a good cop usually didn't pay off. Good cops usually ended up sitting at the bottom of the pile, getting transferred, or lying in a hole six feet under; more often than not, the latter. But Toni had persevered, and somehow through his hard work and stubborn tenacity over the past two and a half decades, he managed to rise up to the rank of Sergeant, slipping past the mayor's fat, stubby nose. After solving the Anniston case six years back, the superintendent had had no choice but to give him a promotion, despite the numerous public clashes he had with the city's corrupt leader.

Toni had settled down a bit now that he had gotten older. He had trouble keeping up with some of the younger detectives. Back in his prime, Rizzo was the bane of every gangster in town, including the mayor himself, but now he was just a tired old man, too poor to retire, but too old to chase the tails of the modern breed of criminal. Most of all, Antonio Rizzo couldn't bring himself to embrace the many advances in technology which often left him trying to drag the mammoth back to his cave while his colleagues had already adopted the wheel.

Even as a boy, Rizzo had little interest in technology, and as the years went by, the tech continued to grow and change, while he continued to look the other way. He had never needed all those expensive hunks of metal with their glowing, beeping buttons to solve his cases. He didn't need a degree in computer science to figure out who was behind a murder. The detective had never needed any of that in the past and he couldn't see why anyone else did either.

For Sergeant Rizzo it didn't stop just there at a lack of understanding, it continued deeper. He had developed a solid hatred for this vast realm of knowledge which lied outside his reach. Sitting atop this mountain of mystery were the robots. For Toni they were proof that mankind had gone too far, that the hubris of man had led them to create beings in their own image, and like when God had created man, these creations were more flawed than the creators had been. Mankind was already flawed enough, the last thing they needed were cheap knockoffs with a near limitless database of knowledge at their disposal.

The sergeant's daughter, Abby, thought he was just a ridiculous old man. She was probably right, he knew, but he was too old and too stubborn to change. His nine-year-old daughter could run circles around him when it came to anything with buttons or a touchscreen, and he knew it would only get worse. Now she was pushing him to buy one of those new holographic user interfaces for the family computer, and he was running out of excuses to say no.

Sometimes his lack of savvy made him feel ashamed, but today he would come home proud. Today was a good day. Today would be the day he proved himself right.

There had been another murder the night before, nothing really out of the ordinary, or so it had seemed. The victim had been a high executive of one of the biggest businesses in country. The call had been made by a young woman who had seemed hardly capable of even remembering her own name. After an initial examination of the crime scene, Rizzo had the girl brought down to the station to take her statement. She had looked like a mouse caught between the cat's paws, but after a bit of gentle coaxing he had gotten her to describe the events of the day.

After taking her statement, the detective began to review the footage from the security cameras outside the victim's office and down at the front desk. What he had found had been like a slice of pure bliss, and he immediately sent a team of patrolmen to make an arrest.

"See, I told you," said Toni over the phone, still giddy with excitement. "I always knew they were no good, and now I've finally got the chance to prove it once and for all."

"I'm happy for you, dear," replied his wife, Melinda. He expected she was probably smiling like she would when Abby saw a drone fly by and called it a fairy, but he didn't care. Toni was in a good mood and nothing was going to sour it right now. "When will you be home for dinner?"

"I'm sorry, hon, but I think I'm gonna be late tonight—"

"Hey Sarge!" called out a voice from the other side of the room.

Blushing slightly, the detective hastily said, "Sorry, honey, I gotta go. I'll talk to you later." Rizzo ended the call and put his phone back into his pocket.

"Sarge," repeated Detective Lawrence, one of the youngest detectives on the force, "they brought that robot in just now. You should see 'im. He's wearing a hat and a coat. You ever seen a robot dressed for autumn before?"

"Can't say I have, Jim. What about the owner, Sinclair? Does that name sound familiar to you?"

"Hm, maybe from those shampoo commercials? The robot claims he's out of town, but he wouldn't say where or for how long. Should we look for him?"

Rizzo considered for a moment before saying, "Put out a BOLO. If anyone sees him I want to know, but for now I'll focus on the machine. Where is it?"

"They put him in Interrogation Room #2. Hey Toni, do you mind if I watch? Just through the mirror."

"Sure," replied Rizzo. Jim was a good kid. He was still accepting bribes, but aside from that he showed some promise. Maybe with a bit of guidance he could be pushed onto the right path.

The sergeant stood up and stretched, his back cracking like thunder. "Ergonomic chair my ass," he cursed under his breath.

The detective picked up a tablet along with his pen and notebook, two relics that made him the butt of many a joke at the station, and marched across the office towards the interview room. Once the blood flowed again into his feet he let a confident strut creep into his gait.

"Hey, Toni, is it Christmas early this year or what?" said Lieutenant Costa with a chuckle as he passed. The sergeant knew he was being made fun of, but soon enough he would be the one laughing.

Rizzo ignored the man and continued by until he reached Interrogation Room #2. The detective opened the door to find a silver robot designed to look male sitting in the stainless steel chair behind the table. It was a dimly lit room with no windows besides the one-way mirror to the android's right. The machine was wearing a tan rain coat and a brown, wool hat. Rizzo stood for a moment in the doorway, taking in the sight before him. He had to fight to prevent a smile from curling beneath his black and grey moustache.

Finally, the detective fully entered the room, closing the door behind him, and took a seat across from the robot. It stared at him calmly with its pale blue eyes. Rizzo had promised himself that nothing would break his good mood today, but somehow the lifeless eyes of these machines always managed to get to him. There was something ominous in that dim luster. Something cold and heartless.

Rizzo tugged at his favorite burgundy vest, smoothening it over his flat belly and then the detective rolled up the sleeves of his white shirt. The machine just sat there silently, watching him, waiting for him to say the first word.

"I'm Sergeant Rizzo," introduced the officer. "You can remember that," he added, not wanting to have to introduce himself again.

"You can call me Seven," replied the machine in a strange, gruff, nasally voice which still retained a slightly tinny tone.

"Seven, do you know why you're here?" asked the Sergeant, uncertain how keen the machine would be. Sometimes they were little more than the mechanical puppets at a children's pizza party venue, and sometimes they were surprisingly astute.

"For the alleged murder of Miles Grayson according to the arresting officers." It would appear this machine stood towards the more perceptive end of the spectrum. Rizzo supposed that was a good thing. Not only would it make this interview less frustrating, but it would be more satisfying to prove that a fully-fledged artificial intelligence was capable of conscious murder than if some giant toy had simply malfunctioned.

"Good," said Rizzo, pausing for a moment. He wasn't really sure where to begin; there weren't really any procedures in place for interrogating robots. "I'll admit this is new for me...why don't you start by telling me where you were last night between 8 and 9 p.m."

"I was in my office trying to make sense of my current case," it replied.

"Your current case? You mean Mr. Sinclair's case?"

"Sure."

"And what case would that be? Did this have something to do with Mr. Grayson and Orion Industries?"

"Yes, I was looking into the possibility that Grayson stole some money from a competitor."

"What competitor?"

"Speculo."

"That's the name of a company?" asked Rizzo as he jotted down the name in his notebook. "Someone from Speculo hired you?"

"That's right."

The officer was beginning to feel that he would have to try to scrape every little bit of information out of this robot. He wondered if this was part of its privacy restrictions or if the machine was just being difficult. "Who hired you and when?"

"The owner, Ethan Willis, approached me yesterday morning at 9:32."

"And then you paid a visit to Mr. Grayson at his workplace?"

"Twice. At 11:23 and at 2:03."

There we were. The sergeant had managed to catch the automaton in a lie, and already so soon in his interrogation. And here he was thinking a computer would be a tough nut to crack.

"You're sure about that? You didn't visit Mr. Grayson three times?"

"I'm pretty good with numbers. I know the difference between two and three. Do you?"

Toni ruffled his brow and wriggled his moustache. Sass from a robot? He wondered fleetingly what he would think of the station's robotic receptionist if it spoke to him with attitude like that. It certainly had the effect of making the machine seem more lifelike.

"So you weren't there between 8 and 9 last night?"

"I believe I already answered that, detective."

The sergeant picked up his tablet computer and pulled open the surveillance footage from the camera positioned outside the executive's door. He handed the device to the robot who was handcuffed to the table. "Maybe this'll refresh your memory. Pay attention to the timestamp there in the corner."

The bionic man examined the footage. Though the detective couldn't see the tablet screen, he had watched the footage so many times he knew every frame. The robot had casually walked into the room at 8:32 p.m., and then eleven minutes later walked back out. Though the machine didn't have any facial muscles, Rizzo could honestly say he had never seen a robot look quite so perplexed before.

Rizzo thought he noticed the robot fidget with its wrist for a moment, but a second later it handed the tablet back to him and said, "I wasn't there last night. Ask the receptionist."

"I did, and funnily enough it didn't seem to remember you at all. I'm pretty sure robots aren't included in the right-to-privacy laws, so it struck me as pretty odd. After that I checked the visitor database and your name isn't listed there. Looks like you cleaned up your tracks after you left, but you forgot about the surveillance cameras.

"Based on what I've pieced together from the camera footage, here's the timeline as I see it. You came in yesterday morning a little after 11 and left with Ms. Harper at a quarter to 12. The two of you returned just under two hours later, but after your second visit to Mr. Grayson, you didn't leave the building. Maybe you thought if you left you wouldn't be allowed back in again later, so you stayed there, lying in wait until your target was alone. At 8:32 you entered Grayson's office and shot him in the head with a 9 millimeter round. I don't know what you did for the rest of the night, but the footage in the foyer shows you leaving this morning at about 7 a.m. just a couple hours before we picked you up at Sinclair's office. Any of this sound familiar?"

"I can't say it does," replied the robot calmly.

"I've spoken with nearly a dozen employees from Orion who can verify that you and the victim had a fight yesterday afternoon and that he was pretty riled up afterwards. Then apparently you were wandering around the office harassing employees for quite some time. Your face is all over the cameras and you left a memorable impression on people."

Seven sat, blank-faced and said nothing.

"You have anything to say for yourself?"

"I can't say that I do."

Rizzo found himself feeling somewhat disappointed. He had expected more from this case. The great victory he had been waiting for all this time had come too easily to savor. There was no game in it.

"So you confess?"

"I didn't say that," replied the robot. "The description of events you've given sounds reasonable, but it's false, and the evidence was clearly fabricated."

"The footage was already checked by forensics and they claim it's genuine."

The robot shrugged. It shrugged as if the officer had simply asked it the time and it didn't have a clock on it. This machine clearly didn't realize that its existence was at stake here, or more likely it didn't care.

Rizzo sighed as he stood up and approached the door. They would need to put the machine in a holding cell for now until they could figure out what the proper protocol is for such a case. Before he left, he took one last look into the room and once again found himself thinking that he had never seen a machine look quite so puzzled.

CHAPTER 11

Seven marched down the shadowy corridor of the 1st district police department alongside his police escort. The officer had been nice enough to chain his hands together so they wouldn't get separated. Every eye turned his way as he passed by. Everyone wanted a peek at the first robot to ever end up in the slammer. What would they do to a robot who had committed a capital offense? Was he destined to rust in the damp corner of some dark, grimy dungeon in upstate Illinois? Or would they simply shut him off and compress him into a little metal cube in the junkyard? Seven had no intention of finding out.

What he did want to find out was how things had ever gotten to this point to begin with. It was clear to him that he had been framed, but why? Seven knew he sometimes rubbed people the wrong way, and there were those who had it out for him just because of what he was, but somehow he doubted that it had been personal. Had someone really been out to get him or had he just been in the wrong place at the wrong time?

Seven needed to decide what his next move would be. Clearly the first item on his agenda was to bust out of this sorry excuse for an establishment of justice. But what would he do after that? He couldn't go back home, that was clear, but what else did he have? There was an old safe house he had seen Vic use once, but who knew if it was still standing. He supposed his primary focus should be on establishing his innocence, but even if he could prove it, what good would it do? At this point he was pretty sure he was destined for the recycling plant regardless of his guilt.

What would Vic say if he could see Seven now? Vic had always given Seven the same freedom he would have given any human. He had had just one rule, just one paramount rule which should never be broken: don't get caught under a cop's magnifying glass. Vic always said the police in this town were more corrupt than a campaigning politician, and that he had left the force to get away from that, so that he could finally do some real good. But that wasn't the only reason he told Seven to stay away from the fuzz. Vic had known that Seven's unique development, unburdened by the limits built into his programming, put both of them at risk.

As Seven considered the sight of Vic's disappointment, he cast his blue eyes downwards as if his lenses had suddenly grown too heavy for his head. A little rectangular, grey cleaning bot scuttled across the floor, hovering about a centimeter above the tiles. The little droid scurried to the edge of the hallway to avoid being stepped on.

"Friend of yours?" teased the cop, thinking Seven had been watching the little appliance.

"Sure, why? You want me to set you up on a date?"

The officer jerked his head around and stared at Seven like a caveman who just discovered fire. "Why you talking so funny?"

"Something must have snuck past my firewalls," replied Seven. "It'll pass."

"Ah yeah." The cop relaxed his bewildered expression like a constipated man finally making a deposit in the porcelain bank. "I think I heard about somethin' goin' around."

They rounded the corner and came to a tan, metal door with a small safety glass window. Beside the door was a panel with a biometric scanner. Seven's escort pressed his hand against the panel which replied with a soft blip followed by a grinding buzz noise. The door slid into the wall and the man and robot stepped through into the new hallway.

The corridor was lined on both sides with metal bars, behind which dozens of men of all shapes, colors, and sizes stood, sat, or slept. Most of the men looked glum, almost as if they could sense that depressingly grey weather they were missing outside. A few approached the bars to get a better look when they saw what was approaching.

The officer came to a halt in front of one of the holding cells and pressed his hand on the scanner beside it. The bars slid open and he looked at Seven, waiting for him to climb into his cage like a good little bird.

"You ain't serious are ya man?" called out a scrawny, bug-eyed man with greasy hair from inside the cell. He had an annoying, hyperactive voice with a distinctly paranoid sound to it. "You can see that's a robot, can't ya man? You can't put no robot in a cell." He turned to face some invisible person behind him and said, "Can you believe this guy? He can't even tell the difference 'tween a guy and a robot."

"Shut your trap, Jitterbug," replied the cop. "This here robot is a cold-blooded criminal just like you. Heh, only his blood's a lot colder 'n yours."

A particularly large man, who Seven thought could probably pick his teeth with a twerp like this Jitterbug, stepped towards the open grate. He was wearing a tight, white tank top, and a particularly busty version of the Statue of Liberty was tattooed on his upper arm.

"Hey, to the back of the cell!" ordered the officer.

"I'm just looking," came back a deep baritone.

"Well look from back there, Sheldon."

"Don't call me that," replied the big man calmly. When a big guy like that expresses dissatisfaction in such a calm way it has a strange, petrifying effect on most people. The guard

64

placed his hand on his sidearm, and the big guy stepped back again.

The officer made a gesture to the android by pointing with his nose and said, "Get in."

Seven stepped inside the cell and then turned around to face the entrance. The bars slid back in place, separating the robot from freedom, but still allowing him to see it from a distance in a taunting sort of way. Seven held out his arms through the bars so the officer could remove his shackles.

"You want somethin' from me bucket head?" said the cop, grinning sardonically.

"You mind taking these off? I just polished those wrists and I don't want them getting scratched up."

"Naw, I think you should keep 'em. They match your complexion, gorgeous." The officer guffawed, clearly thrilled by his clever jape. He turned and walked away, whistling an upbeat tune to match his footsteps.

There were four men in his cell, and they converged on him all at once, all curious about this silver man who had somehow ended up in the same place as them. After a few seconds, Jitterbug lost interest and started talking to himself, but the others continued to look him up and down.

"I have never seen a robot with a coat before," commented the big man who didn't want to be called Sheldon in his deep, slow, monotonic voice. "It is a nice coat."

"Thanks," replied Seven, not really sure what else to say.

"So what are you in for?" droned the big man.

"I asked the mayor if he was pregnant or just fat," replied Seven, not wanting to have a cliché 'I'm innocent' conversation.

"Really?" replied the man, sounding almost impressed.

Seven continued to entertain his cellmates for a little while longer, but in the background he had already started getting to work. During his interview with Sergeant Rizzo, the detective had made the mistake of handing Seven his computer. The android had taken advantage of the opportunity to plug himself into the device and install a backdoor. The sergeant had almost caught him in the act, but fortunately Seven had been quick enough to dissolve any suspicion.

Seven climbed through his backdoor into Rizzo's workstation, and from there he entered the department's network. He spent the better part of an hour probing and scanning until he found what he was searching for: the programmable logic controller. This was essentially the heart of the station's entire control system, regulating everything from the ambient temperature to the security doors in this wing of the building. Access to the PLC should never be exposed to the Internet, and whoever had set it up had at least done that right, but they had been lazy when it came to isolating it from the internal network. It was clear that they had never needed to detain an android before today.

Unfortunately the PLC was not one of the models Seven had practiced playing with back at the Sinclair office, but after a little research online he discovered a zero-day vulnerability in the firmware which was made public a year ago, and had been quickly patched. Fortunately for Seven, the precinct's administrators were lazy and had neglected to install the updates. A few minutes later he was in. Seven was confident he would be able to work with this.

Now he just needed a diversion. He was fairly certain that there were still far too many patrolmen roaming the station to make his move just yet. Seven checked the public stream from the CCTV camera across the street from the station and confirmed his prediction. Still far too many squad cars in the parking lot outside the building.

The android began making some phone calls, each time routing the connection through a different proxy to make it appear as though the calls originated from different numbers. Each time he transmitted a different voice, sometimes making something up himself, sometimes borrowing a little snippet from Hollywood. A civil dispute up on Randolph Street, a mugging in Millennium Park, a bank robbery in progress on West Madison Street, a major drug deal down by the docks, the list went on. Seven continued his calls, watching the camera feed as the vehicles slowly disappeared from the parking lot.

After nearly an hour, Seven decided that he wasn't likely to reduce the numbers any further, and if he waited much longer they would figure out that they had all been sent on a wild goose chase. It was time. Seven unlocked the door in the hallway and it slid open, buzzing angrily, cranky for being yanked out of its slumber. The other captives all turned to look, irritated by the lack of an officer. Next, Seven opened the cell doors. All of them.

"Whoa whoa whoa!" said Jitterbug, bouncing up and down like an unbalanced washing machine.

A few men whooped in the cell across from Seven's, and one or two men immediately ran, not taking the chance that the doors would close again. Most stood and waited, looking suspiciously.

"Sh-should we make a run for it?" asked a young man in the cell to Seven's left.

"You think it's a trap?" asked another. "Like…like do you think they opened all the doors and whoever tries to make a break for it gets an extra two years on their sentence?"

"That could happen," confirmed Jitterbug, who Seven doubted had any legal expertise. "I've seen it. They can do that. It happened to my buddy Jerry last summer. Cops these days'll do anything."

"Well I am going," asserted the big guy. "Who is coming with me?"

"I've downloaded the blueprints for the building," stated Seven. "If you go through that door and take a left, walk to the end of the hall, and then take another left it'll bring you to the entrance."

The big man smiled and said, "Thank you, robot. You are a good robot." Then he patted Seven on the head like a small dog, lightly tapping the android's hat with his palm.

The big guy stepped out of the cell and confidently walked through the metal security door while the others meekly followed him. Seven remained in his cell until he was alone, and then casually strolled after them, taking a right instead. The android hadn't lied to them, the directions he had given would indeed lead to the entrance, but it would also take them past all the offices which were bound to have a few officers still present. Seven had elected to take the back door which he judged to be far less risky.

The detective walked down the hallway, listening closely for any sign of trouble. Somewhere behind him he heard the faint din of shouting. So far, so good. But when Seven rounded the corner he saw a young female officer looking down, focused on the tablet in her hands. Seven had no time to hide, so instead he used his connection to the station's infrastructure to turn out the lights in the hallway and then he disabled the backlight behind his eyes so he wouldn't be visible in the darkness. He would be rendered essentially blind, but he had already seen the corridor, and he had the floor plans, so he was confident he would be able to navigate the rest of the way.

"What the?!" shouted a female voice which was followed by a thud and a groan as the girl tripped and fell, her glowing tablet skidding across the floor.

Seven carefully sidestepped to avoid the place where he had last seen her and he continued down the hall.

"Hello? Is somebody there? What's going on?" The voice was a short ways behind him now.

The android continued silently, and after 19 meters he pivoted 90 degrees and entered the next hallway. This would be the final stretch. The android reactivated his optical senses and was now within sight of the outside world. He pushed open the doors and exited into the black urban night. He made it. Seven wondered if Vic would be proud if he had witnessed his great escape. He thought so.

It was dark outside, or at least as dark as it ever gets in a city like Chicago which is most alive in the depth of night. A light drizzle fell from the clouds above which blotted out the moon, but compensated by reflecting the light from the skyscrapers. Seven could hear sirens in the distance, a sound which was most noticed by the typical city-dweller only in its absence.

Seven took a sharp right, following the exterior wall of the building, not wanting to cut across the parking lot which may soon be refilling. Just as he reached the street he nearly collided with a large moving object.

"Oh, it is the robot," came a slow, deep, drone. It was the big man from his cell, and beside him was Jitterbug, nervously jerking his head around, expecting someone to jump out and grab him at any second.

"Looks like you made it out," said Seven. He had not expected them to escape.

"You are a good robot. You come with us."

"I don't think that's such a good idea," replied the detective.

"You helped us, now I help you." He pointed at Seven's still cuffed hands.

"Well..." said Seven. He did need to get those cuffs removed somehow, and he did need a place to charge for the night. He couldn't go back home; that's the first place they'd look for him. "Alright, lead the way."

CHAPTER 12

"Let me get this straight," summarized Seven as he followed his unusual new bedfellows while his hands dangled uselessly in front of him, "you broke into a house and the alarm went off, and when the security firm called to ask if everything was fine you answered the phone?"

"Yes," replied the hulk smiling into stupid oblivion. Somehow he didn't appear to be bothered by the cold despite being severely underdressed for a midnight stroll in November.

"And you told them your name?"

"Yes."

"And when they told you to wait there until they arrived that didn't raise any red flags for you?"

"I didn't see any flags, no."

"Alright, let's start over. What's your name, big guy?"

"Sheldon."

"I thought you didn't want to be called that?"

"I don't."

Clearly this guy was operating on a severely underclocked processor. Seven looked to the scrawny man walking beside the goliath and said, "Do we have some sort of language barrier between us? Come on, help me out here Jitterbug."

Jitterbug shrugged and said, "This happens every coupla weeks, but he always get off with a warning because he's Caesar's cousin. The boss just passes a little money around to the right people and they sweep the whole thing under the rug."

Suddenly Sheldon stopped, exhaling with the reverence of a man beholding Eden, and pointed, "There it is."

Just ahead stood an old, derelict brick building that looked like it had already been swallowed by the city and partially digested. The once red bricks had turned a grungy black color, and the building was almost completely devoid of glass where the windows were supposed to be.

"Aw man, I thought we were going to the good safe house," complained Jitterbug.

"This is the good one," replied Sheldon with a look of satisfaction.

The giant stepped forward and reached up to grab the metal ladder from the fire escape and pulled it down. He and Jitterbug quickly climbed up. It took Seven significantly longer to reach the top with his hands bound together.

At the summit of the four storey building, the two inept gangsters had already climbed through the gaping hole in the wall. Sheldon was talking to someone using a phone which had been stashed away beneath a loose floorboard while Jitterbug was talking to a photo on the wall. Seven was beginning to doubt the wisdom of allying himself with these two.

The room was dark and covered in a thick blanket of dust, giving everything a drab, grey tint. An old, probably green sofa stood in the center of the room and a bunk bed sat in the corner. Other than that the room was completely empty. The only signs of life were the cat paw prints going in both directions between the sofa and the window they had come in through.

"Okay, thanks, Jimmy," said Sheldon, hanging up. "He says he'll be here in half an hour."

"Oh man. What're we supposed to do for half an hour, man?" asked Jitterbug.

"You got someplace to be?" Seven asked. Jitterbug pouted but went back to mumbling to himself. Sheldon sat down on the sofa and stared at the wall. The android was beginning to feel like the most human one in the room.

Seven passed the time thinking about Vic, wondering if his mentor had ever gotten himself into such a mess during the course of his long career. Vic never liked to talk much about his past, but those rare gemstones he did reveal were stored as close to the android's figurative heart as possible. He had instantly adopted them as core memories, the type of runtime-level programming which helped to shape his fundamental values.

Twenty minutes later a short, middle-aged man wearing a puffy black coat and a beret cap climbed through the window carrying a black leather bag and saying, "Knock knock."

"Jimmy!" exclaimed Sheldon gleefully like a little girl who just spotted a pony. He ran forward and embraced the man in a spine-crunching bear hug.

"Yeah yeah, nice to see you too, kiddo," replied the man whose name was apparently Jimmy.

Jimmy walked into the center of the room and set down his bag on the couch and opened it up. "I'm gonna take a wild stab in the dark and say you're the robot," he said in a sarcastic tone looking at Seven.

"You're pretty sharp," replied the detective.

"That's what my mother always tells me," he replied, enjoying the playful banter. A second later he produced a tablet and a small, black, rectangular device with a cable attached to it. He plugged the device into the computer and then pressed the other end against the electronic lock on Seven's handcuffs. "Hold still now."

Seven watched the computer screen as a series of letters and numbers spanned the interface. Jimmy tapped a few buttons and the characters began to cycle rapidly, running through thousands of combinations until finally landing on a frequency which resonated with the particular lock responsible for Seven's current disability. Suddenly the cuffs popped open and Seven was free.

"There you go, guy. Free as the day you rolled off the assembly line."

"Thanks a lot," said Seven, making an effort to sound grateful. It was an emotional response he didn't often have the occasion to flex.

"Hey, you did my boy, Shelly, a solid, so it's the least I could do. You need anything else just holler."

It's a funny world where you can get more courtesy and honor out of a bunch of mobsters than the cops. Seven didn't want to push his luck, but he actually did have something in mind, and he hoped the man might be able to help him out. "Well, there is one thing. I guess I'm probably a wanted man right now, and if I use my credit card I'll be watching a pretty parade of red and blue lights within a few minutes. Any idea where I could get my hands on a less conspicuous card?"

"You're in luck, buddy. I got you covered." Jimmy pulled out a different device from his bag of tricks and plugged it into his computer. The man stuck a gold-colored plastic card into the device, and a moment later he said, "Voila! Here you go. That there's a prepaid card with enough cash on it to last you for at least a couple days unless you're some kinda hedonist. Nobody's gonna bat an eyelash at that one."

"Wow, you're a lifesaver, Jimmy. Where'd the money come from?"

"It's better if you don't know."

Changing the subject, Jimmy raised his voice to catch the attention of Jitterbug who was wandering around the back of the room near the beds. "Alright, listen up. Now that the main business is taken care of, I'll need to report back to Caesar to let him know what's going on. You three just lie low here for the night. I brought you guys some provisions." He reached once more into his bag and pulled out a six-pack of beer and two blankets.

Sheldon's face lit up and he said, "Jimmy, you're a good friend."

"I know, big guy. So you kids just sit tight and tomorrow I'll pick you up." Turning to Seven, he said, "You coming with tomorrow, Silver?"

"You're talking about Caesar, as in the big gangster?" asked Seven.

"Sure," replied Sheldon, sounding confused. "What other Caesar is there?"

"Thanks for the offer, but I think I'll pass. Tomorrow I've got a full day ahead of me." Or at least he would as soon as he figured out exactly what his next move would be. Seven had entered new territory, and Vic wasn't around to guide him through it this time.

"Suit yourself," shrugged Jimmy.

Jimmy took up his tools and left the way he came in, and Seven's two roommates polished off the six-pack and then went to bed. Sheldon's thundering snores threatened to shake the flimsy building down to rubble. Seven spent the night deep in thought.

What was he supposed to do next? He didn't like just sitting around, wasting his time, but it wasn't considered socially acceptable amongst the organics to disturb them in the middle of the night, so as much as he disliked it, he would need to wait until morning to make his next move. He had still yet to reach his client, so he supposed he would try calling him once more first thing in the morning.

But perhaps more pressing were the circumstances of his own framing. Clearly whoever had set him up knew how to manipulate the camera footage, and somehow that person had obtained access to it. Kaminski was the first name that sprang to mind. Not only would he have the technical finesse to fabricate the evidence, but he would have the skills to tap into the system, and maybe even inside knowledge about how it's all set up.

Seven was still uncertain what exactly was afoot here, but he hoped that tomorrow would shed new light on it all.

CHAPTER 13

Seven disappeared early the next morning before his companions awakened. He knew he ought to ditch his signature coat and hat, knowing that without them he could easily blend into the crowd, but somehow he couldn't bring himself to do it. Vic had given him those items after their first case together, telling him, "See Seven, you're a bona-fide private eye now." Seven struggled with an inner tug-of-war between logic and this unknown force at work within him as he took a car to the apartment of Max Kaminski. Along the way, he had attempted once more to reach his client, Ethan Willis, on the phone, but once again there was no answer. He resolved to pay the programmer a visit and then he would drop by Willis's office in person.

The sky mourned summer's passing, shedding cold tears and wheezing heavily, forcing Seven to hold onto his hat to keep it from blowing away as he walked across the sidewalk to the front door of the decrepit building. A few moments later the detective stood outside Kaminski's door and knocked. When there was no reply, he tried once more, and this time he heard a despaired wail followed by a violent roar of anger from within.

The door swung open and a man stood there in his boxers and t-shirt. He was wearing a headset with a lens over his left eye and a microphone in front of his mouth. "What!?" he barked angrily.

"Morning, Max," replied the android. "Got a minute to chat?"

"Ugh," he groaned, as he walked back into the room, leaving the door open. "This better be important. You just killed me."

Inside the room was a semi-circle of holographic images obfuscating three walls. The holograms depicted a sort of military facility with soldiers patrolling the perimeter. Kaminski took a position in the center of the room and formed his hand into a gun shape, pointing it at the hologram. As he did so, the images burst into life, becoming more vivid and animated.

"So, Max," began Seven, "I guess I'll start by asking you where you were on Tuesday night between 8 and 9 p.m."

"Aw, come on, seriously?" complained the programmer. "Stupid goddamned bots."

"Excuse me?"

"I know, right?" Max replied, sounding amused. "Okay, you go around to the bunker and I'll try to scale the building. We can meet inside."

"Are you talking to me?" asked Seven.

"No," said Kaminski in an annoyed tone, this time turning his head to look at the detective. "Can't you see I'm in the middle of something?"

"I've got a lot on my plate today, so I'd appreciate some focus. The sooner you answer my questions, the sooner I can be on my way."

Kaminski pulled his invisible trigger and put a hole in a man's skull. "Look, you're pretty interesting for a robot, I'll give you that, but your impatience is just a programmed response, it's not real. So just stand there and stop distracting me until I'm at a good place to stop."

"My impatience is a direct response to your rude behavior."

The programmer sighed loudly and said, "I like robots, really. I spend most of my day everyday talking to computers, but the thing is I know how you work. Everything you say and do is just the sum of a lot of very clever programming." He loaded an invisible clip into his hand and resumed firing.

"Are you really any different?" asked the robot, his patience wearing thin. "Humans come loaded with firmware in the form of genetic code and they're then programmed over the years by parents, teachers, society, and experiences. It's the same thing. So could you cut the crap and show me a little courtesy?"

Kaminski turned away from the display and the game paused. "You want courtesy? Why do you think you deserve to be treated like a real person?"

"Because I want to be. Does there need to be anything more?"

The programmer made a puzzled expression and looked away, staring at the wall for a moment. Finally he groaned loudly and took off his headset, placing it instead around his neck. "Fine, but make it quick."

"Good. Where were you Tuesday night?"

"Here playing video games."

"For how long?"

"The whole night, man. Why?"

Seven ignored the man's question and asked, "What do you know about Orion's security systems?"

"Nothing," shrugged the man unconvincingly.

"You sure?"

"Yeah I'm sure. Why are you nagging me?"

"If someone were to dig down they wouldn't find any traces of entry into Orion's network from unauthorized sources? Maybe from someone by the name of 'headbanger46'?"

Kaminski's bloodshot eyes opened wide, looking like a greasy, over-caffeinated owl. "W-w-where'd you hear that name?"

"Took me about five minutes to find it when I searched for your email address. So what's it going to be? You ready to confess?"

"Look man, I don't know what you're talking about," said Kaminski with a pained expression, shifting his weight from one foot to the other like he desperately needed to relieve himself.

"You seem to be pretty handy with a gun. Ever held a real one?"

"Once or twice…" he replied meekly. After a moment of hesitation, his aggressive nature bubbled to the surface once more and he barked, "What the hell is this?"

"You know," tested Seven.

"No I don't! If I did I wouldn't have asked."

Seven studied the man's features as he spoke. He didn't appear to be lying, but it was difficult to say for sure. "Grayson is dead."

"What!?"

"He was shot in the head Tuesday night between 8 and 9 p.m."

"Holy shit…" Kaminski turned away and ran a hand through his oily hair.

That seemed like a normal response. Seven was programmed to read human emotions and to understand people, but sometimes he doubted his abilities. You can algorithmically map the motion of an object through space; physics is imperial. Human responses are not so simple. Humans are chaotic systems, perhaps even more random and complex than the weather. The best Seven could ever really do was make an educated guess.

"You didn't know anything about it?"

"No! Are you accusing me of something?"

"I'm just asking the same questions the police are going to be asking sooner or later."

Suddenly the man's eyes widened once more and the fear returned to his face, like a pale, sweaty mask. It was as if the gravity of the situation had just hit him. "I didn't know. I swear, I didn't have anything to do with it."

"Do you know anything which might point to the person who did it?"

"No, I don't know anything. I was here the whole night." Suddenly he narrowed his eyes in suspicion. "Why are you talking to me about this instead of the cops?"

"The cops are slower than I am. Grayson's corpse didn't hand out a big enough bribe to get them moving quicker."

"They don't have anything, do they?" he replied with a smirk.

"Let's get back to the security system."

"Fine," said Kaminski, his confidence now fully restored. "Orion's security is pretty weak. Embarrassingly weak in fact."

"Does that go for the security cameras as well? What would it take to modify the footage?"

"Any script kiddie could manipulate the footage if they knew where to look."

The detective asked, "What kind of access would be required for that? Could it be done from outside?"

Kaminski shrugged, "If you had a way in you could do it from outside. There are ways in. There's a dev server where we test things out and show things to clients and project managers, and it's publicly accessible, just secured with basic auth. Most of the time the credentials are just 'admin:123abc'. You could do a lot from that server."

This was not good news. This meant that literally anyone could be responsible for framing Seven, and if it wasn't Kaminski then the detective was back to square one.

After a short moment of silence, the programmer said, "If you're finished now, I have to get back to work."

"Work?" asked the detective, confused.

"Yeah man, I earn pretty good money live streaming my gameplay."

"You said you were playing Tuesday night," recapped the detective. "Were you streaming then too?"

"Sure, look me up on Gemini.stream. My nick is GutBlaster5000."

As Seven walked back onto the street he checked out the programmer's alibi. According to the timestamps on the site, he was streaming from 5 p.m. until 2 a.m. There was always the possibility that the timestamps were tampered with or that it was actually some other person playing, but for now the detective decided to accept the evidence at face value. That meant his prime suspect was in the safe zone for now and it was back to the drawing board for Seven.

The detective still didn't understand how a simple theft had escalated into murder and how he had ended up in the center of it all. It was time to pay Ethan Willis a visit. The detective was going to get some answers, one way or another.

CHAPTER 14

Seven hailed a cab and made his way over to Cicero just west of Chicago where the office of Speculo was located. The detective spied the wholly average-looking building just ahead through the front window of the vehicle. The three-storey building looked neither old, nor new; it was neither beautiful, nor ugly; it wasn't stylish from the design, but not completely plain either. The building was simply ordinary and unexceptional in every sense of the word. It wasn't negative in any aspect, but rather completely neutral. Somehow that was worse.

As the car pulled up to the curb and slowed to a stop it announced, "Now arriving at your destination. Thank you for using the Chicago public transit. This drive has been brought to you in part by Liberty Firearms: Keeping America free by keeping you armed."

Sure, 'free'. Seven was forced to blend into crowds whenever he saw a cop and to shy away from the cameras because some punk with a gun decided to play target practice with a guy's head. He felt real free right now. Seven was sure Grayson was feeling the freedom as well.

The hatch opened and the detective stepped outside. The rain had let up, but it was still overcast. The smog was thicker than usual today, and the National Weather Service issued another three-day health advisory recommending that people with heart or respiratory problems should avoid any intense outdoor activities. It was times like these that Seven was glad that he didn't need to breathe. Unfortunately he would have to clean his vocal unit yet again at the end of the week to remove the black soot that accumulated. Too bad environmental regulations are worse for business than health risks are. In fact, the there was good money to be made in the health industry.

For a moment Seven hesitated, wondering if he was in the right place. There was no name posted outside the building, and the door was also unmarked. This was the address posted on their website though, so the detective pulled open the door and walked inside.

"I'm looking for Speculo," Seven stated to the receptionist.

"Third floor," she replied.

At least that meant he was in the right building, but he had somehow expected more. Just one floor of this little building? Willis had made it out to be the next big thing, and it had been enough to attract the attention of Orion Industries as well as the scorn of Miles Grayson. But he supposed they were still young and you had to start somewhere.

When he reached the third floor he finally found what he had been expecting: a giant banner with the word Speculo written on it, the 'o' looking like the end of a spyglass. The inside of the building looked much more inviting than the outside. It was clean and fairly modern with chic furniture and good taste in art.

"Hi there, welcome to Speculo," hailed the robotic secretary in a buoyant, enthusiastic tone. "How can I help you?"

"I'm looking for Ethan Willis," stated Seven.

"Oh, I'm sorry, but Mr. Willis is in a meeting right now, but I can leave him a message if you want."

"You do that," said the detective. He wandered over to the snazzy, abnormally-shaped black couch and sat down. "Tell him his private eye is here. I'll just wait here until he's available."

Seven had had enough of Willis's supposed busy schedule. He wanted answers and he wasn't going to leave until he got them. He just hoped that the police hadn't already informed the public about him, otherwise the receptionist may already be making the call. The detective hoped the little bit of chaos he left behind in their network would keep them busy for a few days.

"Sure thing," replied the fembot in a voice that made her sound like a teenage girl. "It could be a little while. Can I get you anything? Something to read maybe?"

"I'm fine, thanks."

The receptionist grinned warmly. She was one of the X-series just like Seven was, maybe just a few versions newer than him. He wondered if she might be like him. He wasn't entirely sure what that meant. Self-aware? Was his near-humanness an attribute that all those of his model shared? Or was it a product of Vic's modifications and his teachings? Or was Seven simply unique? As the receptionist continued to stare at him, grinning like a woman with electrodes attached to her face, he decided she was definitely not like him.

Finally, after 47 minutes of waiting, Ethan Willis made an appearance. He was wearing a shabby, green tweed suit, a white shirt, and a red tie. Looking like a cheap Italian flag, the man approached Seven and held out his hand, saying, "Mr. Sinclair, I didn't expect to see you again so soon. What can I do for you?"

Seven shook the man's hand and replied, "There have been some, let's say interesting, developments in your case. I was hoping you could enlighten me a bit."

"Of course. Let's go somewhere a little more private. There's a meeting room here around the corner."

The businessman led Seven down the hall past a meeting room with a glass door. The room was occupied, and about half the people sitting at the table were bluish holograms. The conference room next door was empty. Willis opened the door and invited Seven to enter.

"So what can I do for you?" asked Ethan cheerfully as he took a seat across from Seven. "How's the case going so far?"

Seven took the man's blissful tone as a sign that he was unaware of Grayson's recent trip to visit the great majority. Or perhaps he was just being coy. "You've been screening my calls. I don't like that."

Willis looked taken aback, having clearly not expected a complaint from a robot. "Sorry, I've been very busy lately, that's all."

"Where were you Tuesday night?"

"I was at a think tank from 6 p.m. until midnight. Why?"

"Can anyone confirm that?"

Willis looked at the detective suspiciously. He clearly didn't like the direction the conversation was headed. "Yes, there were four others from Speculo with me and about 30 other people from all over the city. What's this all about? I'm not sure I like your tone."

"Has there been anything about Orion Industries on the news today?"

"There was something about a police investigation undergoing, but no details." With an impatient, almost urgent tone he demanded, "What's going on? Just come out with it already."

"Miles Grayson is wearing a pine overcoat as they say. Someone put a bullet through his skull Tuesday night between 8 and 9 p.m. You don't know anything about that?"

"What!?" Willis exclaimed, stiffening his back and placing his hands on the table instinctively in case he needed to stand up quickly.

"A strange coincidence that someone decided to feed him a lead sleeping pill the very same day you came to me with a case against him. A little too much of a coincidence for my tastes."

The businessman sat there slack-jawed for a moment, staring forward without really seeing. Seven wondered fleetingly if the man had gone catatonic, but finally his face became animated once more. "I...hmm..." He managed to pull his lower jaw back up where it belonged, and his cognitive abilities seemed to return to him, a sharpness reappearing in his blue eyes. "Why would I hire you to investigate the man if I knew he was going to be dead by the end of the day?"

It was a good question; one Seven didn't yet have an answer to. Of course Willis could just as well be innocent. His reaction had been no less convincing than Kaminski's had. Had it all really been some freak coincidence? What were the odds?

"And like I said," stressed Ethan, "I was at this think tank in northern Chicago all night, and I've got over 30 people who can confirm that."

"After my first meeting with Grayson I was jumped in an alley by a man with a gun and a scrap of paper with my name on it. It was signed with Grayson's initials. I'm not sure why; maybe to lure me back to Grayson's office. But if there was a hitman hired to attack me, the same guy could have done the deed with Grayson. In that case an alibi doesn't mean much."

Willis was beginning to look annoyed. Or perhaps outraged was a better word for it. His cheeks were flushed and a line spanned across his forehead. "What the hell is this? I'm not paying you good money to toss accusations at me."

Seven shrugged. "You haven't paid me anything yet."

Ethan's nostrils flared and he pressed his hands on the table as if trying to force the object down to the second floor. "Why am I talking to a robot actually? Where is Mr. Sinclair?"

Seven was losing him far too early in the conversation, and he still had more he needed to ask. Perhaps he had miscalculated. Had he come on too strongly? He somehow always seemed to forget that what worked for Vic wouldn't necessarily work for him, being a machine. "Mr. Sinclair is currently investigating elsewhere and has sent me to talk with you since I took the initial case summary. I apologize if I came across as rude."

Willis relaxed slightly and sighed loudly. "You mentioned a 'hitman'. I'm sure if this thug was the one who shot Grayson then the police will find evidence on the security cameras. That place is full of them."

The cameras. They were another piece of the puzzle which Seven still needed to work out. Who had manipulated the cameras? How had they done it, and why? "It seems someone tampered with the footage, so all it tells us is that there was someone involved who knew their way around the network."

"Look, I was in meetings here all day on Tuesday and I travelled together with my colleagues from here to the brainstorming session across town where I stayed the whole evening. I was never alone the entire day. When should I have orchestrated all of this? I really don't understand why you're trying to pin it on me now. Is this how you treat all your clients?"

Maybe he was telling the truth. It was hard to say with any reasonable level of confidence. For now Seven would have to just accept his word with a grain of salt and continue his investigation. "You're right, that was unprofessional of me. I am just a robot after all." Willis seemed to calm himself and relax his posture once more. "There's one thing you could do to help with the investigation. I'd like to take another look at your computer in case there's something I missed. Maybe some clue left behind by whoever infiltrated your system."

By the end of the detective's request the man's face had reddened once more and he shifted uncomfortably in his seat. "Well, here's the thing. I'd like to help you, but I can't. I lost it."

"You lost it? The computer you mean?"

"On my way home from the think tank on Tuesday night I cut across the park and I was mugged. He punched me in the gut and then stole my satchel bag." Willis placed a hand over his liver as if experiencing a memory of the pain.

"Did you file a report with the police?"

"Well no…I didn't think they'd actually do anything about it so I didn't bother wasting my time."

"What did your attacker look like?"

"It was pretty dark, but he was wearing a puffy coat and a black mask. He didn't say anything, but he was carrying a gun. I think he maybe had blue eyes? I couldn't swear to it."

This was all becoming stranger and stranger the further down the rabbit hole the detective went. Willis had come to him Tuesday morning, and after meeting with Grayson, Seven had been attacked by a masked man in an alleyway. Then Grayson is killed in the night and a few hours later Willis is attacked by a masked man in a park. Could it have been the same masked man? What were the chances? And yet, what were the chances that all these events had happened independently of each other? Assuming the hitman and the mugger were one and the same, what had been the motivation to steal Willis's bag? Who had hired this hitman and why? And what was Seven's role in all of this? Was he a pawn being manipulated, or was he a wildcard who had somehow gotten caught in the middle of something?

All he knew was that he needed to find that computer. Something had made that bag worth stealing, and Seven wanted to know what it was. He needed to track the thing down, and he was pretty sure he knew just how to do it.

CHAPTER 15

Sergeant Rizzo took another sip of his steaming coffee while he sorted through the mess of papers spread over his desk. The coffee machine always brewed the black beverage far too hot, but at this point the detective's tongue was so calloused that he hardly noticed it anymore. No milk, no sugar, and scalding hot, just the way he liked it.

After the system failure and the jailbreak yesterday, most of the cops at the station had been content to just shrug it off and move on. They were prepared to just chalk it up to a bug in the system and they weren't too concerned about the six offenders who managed to slip through their fingers. Rizzo was the only one who gave a damn, so that meant he was stuck with all the paperwork which needed to be filled out by hand since the network was still on lockdown.

The detective liked to see the world the same way he took his coffee: weakly filtered, unsweetened, and black as sin. It didn't earn him a lot of friends in this town, but Toni Rizzo refused to let anyone pull the wool over his eyes. The others may be willing to accept that it was a random coincidence, but not Rizzo. The detective was certain that the robot had somehow orchestrated the whole thing. He wasn't sure how, but it was too strange of a coincidence. Unfortunately Rizzo lacked the necessary skill to prove it.

"Hey Toni, this must be like the best week ever for you, huh?" mocked Lieutenant Costa, his mouth curled into a sardonic grin. The man's shiny, smooth face looked like it was formed from wax, and there was something so incredibly punchable about it. Rizzo fought to resist the urge. "First you get to arrest a robot and now you get to file reports on actual paper. Careful, if you get any more surprises I'm not sure if your heart can take it." He cackled and walked off.

That was already the third time Costa had passed by his desk, clearly for no other reason than to harass him. The man was clearly bored; the whole station was. With the network down, suddenly no one seemed capable of working anymore. Had they all forgotten how to think for themselves? Rizzo supposed the one silver lining in this whole situation was that it leveled the playing field for him. In fact, he was now at an advantage since he seemed to be the only one capable of operating without his computer.

After a few hours of paperwork and about a liter of coffee, the detective leaned back in his chair, groaning from the stiffness in his back. He sighed and stroked his thick, black moustache absentmindedly. He was frustrated that he had finally managed to catch one of those accursed, heartless machines red-handed and it had somehow managed to squirm its way out of his grasp like some slimy, spineless worm. But at the same time he had to admit he was almost glad. He had initially been disappointed how easy it had been to catch the machine, but now that it had somehow cracked their security and slipped away that meant the hunt was on. The robot just might turn out to be a satisfying opponent yet.

Deciding he needed a change of scenery, Rizzo got up to check on the status of the network. IT had been working all night to figure out what had happened and to get things running again. The detective walked across the building to the server room and knocked on the open door as he stepped through it into the cool, air conditioned room.

"Afternoon boys," greeted Rizzo.

"Hey Toni," replied Murphy, their senior IT guy, taking a massive bite out of a particularly sloppy meatball sub, looking like he only learned to feed himself yesterday. He had a thick marinara moustache and a big red splotch on his white shirt.

"How's the, uh, reboot coming along?"

"Oh it'll still be a while," the techie said with his mouth full.

"How long is 'a while' exactly?"

"At least the rest of the day."

"Alright, that's fine by me," admitted Rizzo. "What about the investigation? Any idea yet what caused the malfunction?"

"Well, so far we couldn't find much. It's hard to say if it was just a bug or a hack. It turns out someone forgot to update the firmware, so there could have been bugfixes or security updates we missed."

"Whose job was it to do that?" asked Rizzo, immediately regretting it when he realized he already knew the answer.

Murphy's face turned the same color as his marinara and he admitted, "Well, mine…"

"Forget I asked; it doesn't matter. Could someone have hacked into our network and opened the doors?"

"Not from outside. Well, at least I'm about 90% sure it couldn't have come from outside."

"What about from inside? Say, a robot who was here in the station?"

"Inside doesn't mean inside the building," replied Murphy, looking like the detective had just told a pretty lame knock-knock joke. "Inside means from within our network. Sure, maybe a robot could have done it if they could get into our network, but even if they could I don't think they're really clever enough to pull off something like this. I mean, look at Cheryl." Cheryl was what the boys and girls at the station had decided to name their receptionist. Rizzo was pretty sure his phone was smarter than that talking heap of wires and screws.

"Do you have access logs for…whatever this thing is we're standing next to?" Rizzo gestured towards the large rack of servers.

"I guess you're talking about the programmable logic controller, not the servers, right?"

"Sure, if that's what makes sense, that's what I meant."

"Yeah, we do, but I didn't see anything really out of the ordinary. Let me check." He set down the remaining half of his sandwich and picked up his tablet. "Let's see, the last person to access it last night was you. You checked status of the cell locks about an hour before the breakout."

"I wasn't here an hour before the breakout, and I have no idea how to look that information up."

Murphy shrugged. "I dunno, but it doesn't really matter. You don't have the privileges to open the doors from your workstation anyway, so it's not like someone could have used your account."

"My account in combination with those missing updates maybe?"

"Hmm, maybe." Murphy shrugged and picked up his sandwich once more and took another bite.

Rizzo sighed and said, "All right, thanks Murph. Let me know if you find anything else."

Back at his desk, the detective slumped into his chair, making an involuntary 'uff' sound, and then began to flip through his notes without really seeing them. Could that robot have somehow used him to break itself free? But how? He had only spoken to the machine for less than half an hour. Was it possible he had somehow leaked his credentials during that time? He was pretty sure he hadn't. He wondered if he was just chasing ghosts. Then suddenly he landed on the most recently filled page: his notes from his interview with Seven Sinclair.

Rizzo jumped up, realizing he had a lead he could follow. "Hey, Lawrence, wanna go for a ride?" he called out to the kid at the desk behind his.

The young detective swiveled around in his chair and his face lit up. "Yes sir!"

Rizzo approached the receptionist at the office of Speculo and produced his badge. "I'm Sergeant Rizzo and this is Detective Lawrence. We'd like to ask Mr. Ethan Willis a few questions."

"Of course," replied the perky humanoid answering machine with an unsettling smile. "I'll let him know you're here. Can I get you anything while you wait? Coffee, tea, water?"

"No," replied the detective, consciously refusing to suffix his response with a 'thanks'.

A few moments later a handsome young man with Nordic features approached the two detectives who were seated on a particularly inefficiently designed couch. The man looked sweaty and out of breath, as if he had run a half-marathon on his way there.

"Sorry to keep you waiting officers," stated the young man. He held out a hand and said, "I'm Ethan Willis. Alice sent me a notification saying you were waiting and I came as soon as I could."

"Alice?" asked Lawrence.

"The receptionist," replied Willis, gesturing towards the grinning metal maniac sitting at the counter behind him.

"I'm Sergeant Antonio Rizzo and this is Detective James Lawrence. If you've got a few minutes, we'd like to talk to you concerning an ongoing investigation we're leading."

"Of course, follow me."

The two detectives followed the young businessman down the hall and into a modern-looking meeting room equipped with holographic projectors on the ceiling, a stylish glass table, and a fascinating piece of abstract art on the wall which appeared three-dimensional and seemed to be moving. Willis took a seat at the far side of the table and the detectives sat across from him. Rizzo pulled a small notebook out of his pocket.

"Mr. Willis—"

"Please, call me Ethan."

"Mr. Willis," Rizzo persisted, refusing to allow himself to become informal with a potential witness, "before we get into details, could you tell us a bit about what Speculo does here and what your role is?"

"It would be my pleasure," said the young man, his eyes lighting up like a virtuoso asked to explain his masterpiece. "Speculo is a small, young business I began last year primarily focused on new innovations in the area of matter replication."

"If you could elaborate…" suggested Rizzo, not wanting to sound ignorant, but unable to think of a clever way to ask for a definition.

"Matter replication," repeated Willis, as if the second time it might suddenly mean something. "Think of it like this: take that pen in your hand. It costs something to produce those; it takes time and materials. But what if you could just stick it in a photocopier and make another like you would with some piece of paper?"

"But that technology already exists, doesn't it?" asked Lawrence.

"Sure, but it only works for certain artificial materials like plastics. But what if you could replicate any object you wanted? You've got a diamond necklace? Why not make it two?"

"But what's it cost?" asked Rizzo, knowing there's always a catch. "You have to have some material in order to make it."

Willis grinned. "Nope, all it costs is electricity. You're thinking conservation of matter, but the whole matter-energy dichotomy is wrong. I won't bore you with all the scientific mumbo jumbo—to be honest I don't completely understand it myself—but basically we've found a way to convert energy into matter."

Lawrence looked fascinated, and Rizzo could tell he was about to get sucked into a sales pitch. Before the young men could continue, Toni asked, "And what's your connection to Orion Industries, and Miles Grayson in particular?"

The businessman's grin went limp and he answered, "Our technology depends on a rare element we can only obtain from Orion. Grayson was against selling to us."

"I see, and that's why you hired the Sinclair Detective Agency to investigate him?"

Willis's face turned pink and he tugged at the collar of his shirt. "I, uh, well I had some Bitbucks and they were stolen. I was hoping Mr. Sinclair could help me recover them."

"And what does that have to do with Grayson?"

"Well, I had a, uh, disagreement with Mr. Grayson not too long ago. He vowed to destroy Speculo, so I thought it was possible he might be behind it." The young man began to perspire like a cold beer on a hot summer day, and he shifted nervously in his seat. "Look, before you ask, I was at a conference on the other side of town all night on Tuesday."

Rizzo and Lawrence exchanged a glance, and then the older detective asked, "What makes you think we're interested in your whereabouts on Tuesday night?"

"That's when the murder took place, isn't it?"

Now Rizzo's curiosity was piqued. The details around the murder hadn't yet been released to the press, and they wouldn't be for another couple of hours. Why did this man know about it?

"That's right," he replied, cautiously. Was this a slip from a particularly incompetent killer? Had this man hired the robot, not to investigate Grayson, but rather to murder him? For now Rizzo would play along and see where this conversation took him.

Lawrence leaned over and whispered, "How's he know about Grayson?"

Rizzo sighed silently. Lawrence should know better by now than to ask a question like that in front of the witness, or perhaps suspect. Ignoring his colleague, Rizzo asked, "Could you tell us a bit about the Sinclair Detective Agency? Who did you talk to there?"

"Well I hoped to talk to the owner, but he wasn't there, so I only spoke to the robot, Seven. A pretty strange sort of bird if you ask me, but he seemed pretty sharp at least." Willis chuckled lightly as if remembering a particularly humorous joke. "It's funny. Actually you just missed him."

"Come again?" said Rizzo suddenly becoming alert.

"Yeah, he just left about an hour ago. He was asking all sorts of stuff about Grayson and Orion and so on."

"What else did he say?"

"Something about cameras. He wanted to know about where I was on Tuesday night. Can you believe my own detective actually accused me of murder?" Willis shook his head indignantly. "But then I suppose he is just a robot after all. You can't really expect any sort of common courtesy from them, can you?"

CHAPTER 16

The modern, two-storey house with white plastic siding stood in the center of a serene, sleepy little neighborhood just outside of Chicago. The interior of the white structure made the outside look like a dirty grey in comparison. The carpet was white, and the walls were whiter. White plastic furniture was neatly arranged along the walls, always perfectly aligned to keep the rooms symmetrical. In the center of the living room stood a large, white leather sofa upon which a young woman sat in her white pajamas. The only reprieves from this white void of nothingness were the brilliantly colored paintings on the walls and the large television display across from the sofa featuring a news report explaining why the growing national debt is no big deal.

If one would look closer, one would find another source of color in the woman's red, teary eyes. Sophie Harper had spent the majority of the past two days crying. She had been forced to take the previous day off while the police questioned her, and she had been unable to work since. She had already called in sick for the rest of the week.

Sophie couldn't recall having ever felt so horrible in her entire life. Without eating and hardly drinking, she simply sat there upon that white sofa staring blankly and disinterestedly at the television. She had been unable to sleep; every time she tried she was haunted by the memory of the look in Grayson's eyes. She was plagued by the memory of his corpse with its head thrown back and that little river of blood flowing down to his lips.

She took a deep breath and sighed loudly. "Pull yourself together, girl."

The young woman extended a shaky hand to take the cup of warm milk she had just prepared from the white coffee table in front of her. She cursed softly as liquid spilled out onto the floor. Sighing, she stood and walked to the kitchen to get a towel.

"This just in," exclaimed an excited anchorwoman, interrupting the previously programmed propaganda. "The identity of the victim in the recent shooting at the Orion Industries headquarters here in Chicago has just been released. The chief financial officer, Miles Grayson, was shot dead Tuesday night. Here's Mitch on-scene. Mitch?"

"Hi Jenna, I'm here outside the Orion Center where the police are still scouring the scene for clues about Tuesday night's butchery. Beside me is Captain Jayden Brown of the 1st district police department. Captain, can you say a few words about the case?"

Sophie wandered back towards her mess, towel in hand, while she stared at the display. She bumped into the back of the couch in her captivated daze.

"Well—Mitch was it?—I can't tell you too much about the case yet. Miles Grayson was killed between 8 and 9 p.m. on Tuesday night. We're still conducting our investigation, but our prime suspect at the moment is an X-series robot who was seen here in the Orion Center exchanging verbal abuse with the victim not long before the time of death. The robot was last seen Wednesday night when he was interviewed by one of my detectives. Since then he's disappeared. Be on the lookout for an X-series robot wearing a tan trench coat and a brown hat."

"Wow, that's really something. I'll keep you updated with more details as soon as we have any new developments here on-scene. For now, back to you Jenna."

Sophie wiped at the wet spot on the carpet while staring in a trance at the TV. Most of the area she was rubbing had not been affected by the spill.

The picture jumped back to the anchorwoman who said, "Thanks Mitch. As some of you may remember, this is the first major crime involving a robot in the last 10 years."

The broadcast froze and a line spanned across the screen with oscillating spikes corresponding with the tone of a soothing, feminine, robotic voice. "10 years ago in the case of Fuller v. Watson, an M-series robot with the appearance of a human congressman was used to bypass security at the Pentagon to steal national security secrets. Would you like to know more?"

"No," groaned Sophie, annoyed. She had meant to disable that feature on her TV because it always interrupted what she was watching with useless information.

The television resumed its broadcast, however the anchorwoman continued to summarize what her TV had just attempted to tell her. Sophie sighed and finished cleaning up her mess. Just as she stood up to carry the towel away the doorbell rang and she nearly jumped out of her skin.

Who could it be? Had her boyfriend decided to drop by after all? She thought not, since he had told her he wouldn't be coming this week. She wasn't expecting any packages or guests. It was after 7 p.m.; too late to be someone going door-to-door asking for donations for their campaign. Perhaps it was the police? She desperately hoped it wasn't, but then again she feared who may have appeared in their stead.

Sophie hugged herself tightly as she nervously inched towards the front door. Standing in front of the white metal slab, she hastily poked one finger against it and just as quickly pulled it away in case it had teeth. A small display appeared on the white void showing the other side of the door through the eye of a small camera. Just outside stood a silver man in a hat and coat waiting patiently.

The girl opened her eyes almost wide enough for them to fall out, and her face went almost as pale as her surroundings. It was that strange robot from the day of the murder, the one the police were looking for. Should she call the authorities? But if she did would it draw her even deeper into this whole mess and maybe even cast suspicion onto her somehow?

In a moment of sudden insanity, she reached out and turned the handle.

"Evening Miss Harper," said Seven amicably.

Sophie opened her mouth to speak but only managed to utter the syllable, "Uh."

"You kids these days talk like cavemen. It's all right, I'll do the talking. Say, do you happen to have VPN access to Orion's network from here?"

"I, uh, yeah."

"Great," said the robot with an unsettling attempt at a smile. He pressed past her into the house without waiting for an invitation.

The android produced a smooth whistling sound and commented, "Nice place you got here. Clearly you business types get paid better than the devs. You've got wildlife though." A white cat with black splotches at the tips of its paws licked itself while eyeing the uninvited guest suspiciously.

Finally Sophie rediscovered the gift of language. "Oh that's Mittens. He's my roommate."

"Sure. I suppose he pays rent too."

The girl hurried over to her baby and picked him up, hugging him protectively.

"VPN?" reminded the robot.

"Uh." Sophie looked around feeling suddenly dizzy and disoriented. After a moment of indecisiveness she set the cat down and went into the office. Another moment later she returned with her computer in hand.

"Great, thanks." Seven took the computer from her hands and turned it on. "Really? No password?"

Sophie stared at him blankly.

"This is why guys like me are stuck with nonsense privacy restrictions." The android shook his head. A few minutes later he had the machine running and he tapped the screen a few times. "Looks like at least Orion knows how to use basic auth. It's says they're using two-factor authentication. You got a phone or something where it sends the code to?"

"Oh, yeah." Like a zombie, Sophie wandered to the living room and retrieved her little pocket computer from the couch. She handed it to the robot.

He activated the device and when he immediately saw her home screen and apps he looked up at her with a scolding expression. "No password." Then he located the code in her messages and continued with whatever it was he was doing.

Sophie was beginning to feel judged. This was her house. Why was she letting this stranger come in and criticize her in her own home? And not just a stranger but a machine. And not just a machine but one that was wanted on suspicion of murder. Why had she let him in at all? What was wrong with her?

"I...I'd like you to go please," she said weakly.

"Sure, I just need a few more minutes."

"No, really I—what are you doing actually?"

"There's a certain virus which I last saw transmitting data to somewhere within the Orion Industries HQ. I'm trying to find the control software."

"Wha...why?"

"So I can see if it's still transmitting."

"I don't understand."

"That's all right."

Sophie stood dumbly and watched him interact with her computer for another 10 minutes until Seven said, "There we are. Pay dirt."

"You found it?" asked Sophie feeling almost excited in spite of herself.

"Sure did, and it's still receiving data."

"What does that mean?"

Seven set down the device which was no longer of any use to him. "It means I can track down a missing computer. Looks like it's transmitting from a hotspot in West Englewood right now."

He stood up and added, "In the mood for a field trip?"

Was he insane? Why should she go to a bad neighborhood at night with a stranger? Was she insane? She was seriously considering going.

Since Seven had arrived she hadn't once thought of that terrible night even though he ought to be a strong reminder. She didn't really believe he was dangerous, and somehow she found him intriguing. Sophie was already caught up in the middle of this whole nightmare; maybe she should see it through to the end.

"I think I'm losing my mind," she said.

"When I'm through with my current case I'll help you find it. Why don't you get dressed."

"Okay," agreed Sophie wondering if she was getting herself into.

CHAPTER 17

The odd couple sat in silence in a dirty cab with a distinctly musky smell. Seven wasn't sure why he had offered to bring the girl with him. She was far more likely to be a hindrance than a help. He wasn't even entirely sure if it had been a conscious decision or the result of some sort of pseudorandomness in his processor.

Perhaps Seven did have his reasons. Perhaps it was something akin to loneliness. Perhaps he simply needed the human touch, that random chaos that only an emotional being can understand. The android could cycle through a million scenarios in a matter of milliseconds and yet Vic always managed to think of something he couldn't. Sometimes Vic's ideas weren't even burdened by the shackles of rational logic, and yet more often than not he turned out to be right. He called it his 'intuition', a phenomenon Seven still didn't understand, and he wasn't certain he ever would.

"What are you thinking about?" asked the girl shyly, interrupting the very thoughts to which she was inquiring.

"I'm thinking about 71 different things right now. You're going to have to be more specific."

Sophie chewed on her lower lip and asked, "How did you know where I lived?"

"You use a professional networking platform and you uploaded your resume to it which displays your contact info in the top right corner."

"Oh," she uttered looking like she felt foolish. "Can I ask you something?"

"You already did."

"Right...anyway, I was wondering...where is your owner?"

"He's not available right now."

"Don't you think maybe you should call him? I mean, you're on the news. The police think you had something to do with Mr. Grayson's death."

"I've got it under control. We're here."

They exited the vehicle onto a pockmarked street lined on both sides with short, two-storey brick buildings. The nearest shop was a prison for cheap liquor with wrought iron bars over the windows. An abandoned garbage truck sat in the parking lot across the street, gutted and harvested of its organs.

"This...isn't what I was expecting," said Sophie nervously as one of her hands attempted to strangle the other.

Seven ignored her and started walking down the dimly lit sidewalk, here and there sidestepping to avoid rubbish which had spilled out of the overflowing garbage cans or to move out of the way of a wandering drunkard.

"Do you know where you're going?" asked Sophie, fear and skepticism clear and strong in her otherwise shaky voice.

"I have a contact in this neighborhood," explained Seven. "I pay her a visit now and then to see what she knows."

"And you think she might know something about this computer you're looking for?"

"No, but it's worth checking. Besides, it's been a while since I last picked her brain."

A few minutes and about 100 meters later the detective stopped in front of a feminine figure standing by the curb facing the street.

"Evening Lucene," greeted Seven.

"Hey there big guy, wanna go for a ride?" replied the figure in a sultry voice as she turned around to face the speaker. She was scantily-clad, wearing only a black latex bra, a red latex skirt, and otherwise only smooth, lightly tanned skin everywhere else. Only her neck and chin revealed the metal exoskeleton hidden beneath her artificial skin.

"Something like that. Why don't we go someplace less conspicuous."

The lustiness went out of the female robot's voice as she said, "Money?" Seven held up his credit card and his counterpart put on a sensual smile, gesturing for him to follow by wriggling her index finger playfully.

After a few minutes, during which time Sophie looked like she wanted to run but was afraid to be alone in this neighborhood, they reached Lucene's nest. It was a dirty apartment with a heart-shaped bed draped with red silk sheets.

Lucene turned around and noticed Sophie. "She costs extra."

"Don't worry about her," said Seven who stepped forward and put his hand on the back of Lucene's neck in a seemingly innocent manner. Suddenly Lucene's playful eyes went dead and her eyelids began to droop.

"Wha-what did you do to her?" asked Sophie, looking left and right as if in fear that someone might see them.

Without moving, Seven explained, "Lucene is an old model with poor security standards and she was never burdened with the new privacy restrictions. She sees a lot of people and they tell her a lot of things, things I'm sure they don't expect her to remember. I drop by about once a month to see what she knows and then I wipe her memory so no one gets the idea that she's a risk."

"You...you hacked into her?" asked the girl sounding mildly repulsed. "But she's a robot like you."

Seven ignored the comment, predicting that if he acknowledged it he would be forced to justify himself. He felt perfectly just in his actions of course, but he wasn't interested in having an ethical debate at the moment. To Seven, Lucene was a lesser being only one step above a car or a computer. She was a tool to be used. And besides that, Seven was convinced that if he hadn't regularly wiped her memory she would have already been discovered by now and shut down.

"Is she a..." Sophie seemed to have lost a word.

"She's what she looks like. She's an object, so it's perfectly legal."

Before the girl could ask any other obvious questions, Seven said, "She hasn't seen anyone resembling our hitman in the past week. Hmm, now that's unexpected."

"What?"

"I've accessed her visual memory, so I see what she has seen, and it seems that she saw Ethan Willis just over an hour ago entering the bar down the street."

"Ethan Willis? He, uh...he was the guy from Speculo, right?"

Seven paused his review of the imagery for a moment to examine the young woman's face. "Where did you hear that name?"

"He and Mr. Grayson had a big fight. Everyone was talking about it in the office." She hesitated for a moment, and with a disgust that somehow overpowered her anxiety, she asked, "You don't think...he wasn't a client of hers, was he?"

"No, but I'm pretty curious why he would be in a neighborhood like this at night, and why he's in the same place as his stolen computer." Seven disconnected himself from Lucene and said, "Come, it's time to find some answers."

"What about her?"

"She'll be fine."

The detective and his sidekick stood outside a brick building with faded white paint and dirty windows covered by a black metal grating. Above the door stood a bright neon sign which should have read "Grady's Pub", but the r, d, and s were still napping. A skinny man who had already seen a long night stood to the left of the door urinating against the wall.

Seven watched as his companion withdrew a small cardboard rectangle from her bag with clumsy fingers. "Do you mind if I smoke?" she asked. She giggled nervously and smacked herself lightly on the forehead. "Of course not, you're a robot."

She inserted a fag between her lips and withdrew her lighter, shielding an infant flame with her hand to protect it from the elements. "I know it's bad for me," she said in preemptive defense. "I only smoke when I'm really tense. It helps me calm my nerves, you know?"

"No, not really," stated Seven as he watched the girl make her contribution to the smog.

"Do we really have to go in there?" she asked, clearly not enthusiastic about the prospect. "Couldn't you at least wait until it's light out?"

"And risk missing my target? And even if Willis and the computer are already long gone, I want to be sure I get into contact with the barkeep who was here at the time."

"Okay, you're right," Sophie conceded unhappily. "Just give me a minute to cool myself."

"Sure."

Sophie took a long, deep huff of black aerosol poison and slowly exhaled. She stared at Seven in a curious way, as if looking at a puzzle or an intriguing work of art. "Hey Seven?"

"Hm?"

"I have a really weird question…I guess it's sorta personal, but I guess you wouldn't mind, right?"

"Shoot."

"Do you think you have a soul?"

Seven absentmindedly cocked his head slightly in the same way his secretarial brethren typically did. He immediately straightened his neck again, agitated by the reflex. "I can't explain what a soul is nor can I logically justify the existence of such a thing, but if they do exist I don't see any reason why I shouldn't have one." The girl gave him an encouraging look, clearly wanting an explanation. "On the premise that all humans have souls and given that babies are humans, if two humans can generate a baby—another human with a soul—that implies that humans can create souls, or at least that their creations can acquire them in some way. Therefore, couldn't a team of humans assemble a machine which possesses one?"

"Huh…" was all the girl said, looking strangely troubled, almost mournful. A moment later she stomped out her cigarette and said, "Okay, I'm ready."

Inside, the walls were red crumbling brick and a long wooden counter divided the room in two, with a dozen rowdy men sitting on stools or at tables on one side and a big-bellied barkeep wearing a black apron on the other side. Behind the barkeep, the wall was lined with row after row of half-empty bottles of liquor.

In the corner, a holographic image of a football game was playing. Someone didn't like the score and threw a bottle at the running-back. It shattered against the wall behind it and the bartender gave the man a good smack, then the two men both laughed heartily.

Seven approached the counter and took a seat on a vacant stool while Sophie glued herself to his back and looked around the room nervously. The barkeep eyed the detective suspiciously. The android said, "Evening. I'll have a beer." He turned his head slightly to Sophie and asked, "You want anything?"

Sophie shook her head shyly.

"You want a beer," stated the barkeep in a tone that said he wasn't amused.

"I want to pay for one," corrected Seven, holding up his card. "You can keep the swill. I just don't want it said that I came in here and took up a stool or your time without buying anything."

The round-faced man pursed his lips and nodded in a satisfied manner, taking Seven's card and charging him for two beers. "So what do you wanna know then, buddy?"

"You got a computer or something on you I could use for a second?"

The tapster looked at Seven suspiciously again but then shrugged and turned around to pick up his tablet, handing it to the android. Seven plugged himself into it and conjured an image of Ethan Willis from his memory.

"Have you seen this man?" asked Seven, handing the tablet back to its owner. "I've got it on good authority that he was here just recently."

The barkeep scrutinized the photo for a moment, his bald head ruffled as he concentrated. "Yeah, I've seen him. He came in here an hour or two ago."

"Was he alone?"

"Naw, he was with a woman. Tall, heavy-chested broad who looked like a blow-up doll. It didn't look like a social call if you ask me. They went into one of the back rooms there."

Sophie shyly interrupted to ask, "Um, sorry, but do you have a bathroom?"

The big man looked down at her with a smirk as if he were looking at a little girl who had inadvertently stumbled into his establishment. "At the end of the hall there."

Once Sophie was gone, Seven asked, "Did you happen to catch a name? Of the woman who was with him."

"Nope, and I didn't care to ask. That lady looked like the type who'd slap a fella in the face with a sexual harassment suit if he annoyed her."

Seven wondered if it could be the person he had in mind. He pointed at the tablet and placed his hand palm-up and wagged his fingers to summon it to him. The barkeep handed him the device. A second later Seven returned it to the barman and said, "This her?"

"Huh, yeah, that looks like her. Friend of yours?"

"Not yet," replied the detective, making a mental note to make Mrs. Grayson's home the next stop on his route. "Are they still here?"

"I definitely saw the lady leave about half an hour ago. Not sure about the guy though. He didn't stand out like she did, so he mighta left and might be he didn't."

"No one else came in with them? Or maybe very soon after? Say a man about 182 centimeters tall with blue eyes?"

The barkeep laughed. "What kinda robot are you? You some kinda detective?"

"That's right."

"Well I'll be damned. Hey Mikey, get a load of this guy." The barkeep slammed a fat fist on the counter in front of a sleeping man sitting a couple of stools down from Seven, the impact causing the glasses on the wooden surface to rattle.

It seemed unlikely he was going to get anything more out of the man. Seven supposed he should be grateful that he had been as cooperative as he had. The barkeep and his drowsy friend guffawed at the strange cosplaying robot.

Motion to Seven's right caught his eye and he turned to bring the dark object into focus. A man in a puffy black coat wearing a black balaclava was attempting to sneak around behind him. Seven stood up fast and lunged towards the man, grabbing him by his jacket. He was quite certain that this was the same man he had encountered right after questioning Grayson.

The masked man immediately began to flail about, and he balled his right hand into a fist and threw it into Seven's jaw. Seven threw his head back to absorb the shock, holding onto his hat with his free hand, while the attacker cried out in pain and recoiled, cradling his hurt paw.

"My turn," said the detective, forming his hand into a miniature wrecking ball and swinging it into the black mask.

The masked man went momentarily limp from the numbing effect of Seven's hook, and he dropped the leather briefcase he had been carrying. A few bystanders cried out in awe at the rare sight of a boxing match involving a robot. Sophie emerged from the toilet, looking confused and startled by the commotion.

Seven grabbed hold of the balaclava, and just before he could pull, the man became alert once more, drew a black pistol from his coat pocket, and aimed it at Seven's torso. The detective quickly pushed the gunman away from him as if he had suddenly grown too hot to touch. The android's metal exoskeleton served as a natural bullet-proof vest, but he didn't want to take any chances. He still had a few vulnerable spots like the eyes, the neck, and his joints, and at point-blank range there was a chance that a bullet could pierce his steel skin.

The gunman fell hard on the ground and his gun misfired, shattering a mirror on the wall. Drunken men dove for cover, upturning tables and throwing mugs down onto the floor. The barkeep stepped into the center of the room with a shotgun in hand and cocked it provocatively. The masked man scrambled quickly to his feet and fled through the front door.

For a moment the formerly rambunctious patrons sat and stared in silence, and nobody moved a muscle. Before the barkeep had a chance to turn his wrath onto him as well, Seven quickly scooped up the masked man's fallen bag, grabbed

Sophie by the arm, and followed the hitman's example, rushing out the door.

CHAPTER 18

The sergeant was feeling guilty for missing dinner yet again. He had called home to apologize an hour earlier, and his wife had been understanding like always, but he knew she was disappointed. It wasn't anything she'd said, or even how she said it, but somehow he could just feel it. Sometimes he had the feeling he ate a fast food supper at his desk more often than his wife's cooking. He wondered if the job was bad for his health.

There was no one forcing Rizzo to put in any overtime. Most of his colleagues had already gone home long ago, but not him. He hated it to leave things feeling so open, like a fresh wound bleeding out. The detective didn't expect to have the whole case wrapped up tonight, but he hoped to at least end the day with some kind of direction.

The network was still down, and he was told it wouldn't be back up until the morning, but he had gotten Lawrence to help him set up a hotspot using his phone with VPN access to the next district's network so he could hunt for traces of that robot in the city's CCTV grid. It was a long and tedious task, made all the worse by the fact that he was unable to leverage the department's facial recognition software on account of the robot having the same face as every other X-series android. He'd already tried and it had brought him nowhere besides three hours into the future. Rizzo had been left with no choice but to configure the search to show him every instance of a person wearing a trench coat and a hat. Remarkably many people in Chicago wear a trench coat and a hat in rainy weather like this.

Rizzo leaned back in his chair and groaned impatiently just as Lawrence showed up looking both tired and excited. "No luck," grumbled Rizzo. "I mean look at this," he jerked a calloused finger at his computer screen, "that's not even a person, it's a bush with a burlap sack caught on a branch. Worthless software."

Lawrence leaned in close and squinted. "I can kinda see it…" He shook his head, remembering why he had come over. "Forget the bush though, I just got news that somebody called in a possible armed robbery in West Engelwood—"

"Forget it, Jim. It's late and I'm tired. Let the dispatcher handle it."

Lawrence's lips curled into a playful smile, like a kid who knows something his teacher doesn't. "It allegedly involves a robot wearing a hat and coat."

Rizzo jumped out of his chair, sending it rolling across the room as he strode over to the coat rack to pick up his jacket. He turned around and said, "Well come on. What are you waiting for? There's a possible armed robbery in progress."

The vehicle pulled over in front of a run-down building in a Chicago ghetto and Rizzo and Lawrence stepped out onto the sidewalk. A squad car was parked alongside the curb with its blue and red lights spinning. Bystanders stared suspiciously at the scene, crossing the street to pass by with as much distance as possible between them and the police.

Inside the bar, the mood was somber. A uniformed officer was questioning the bartender while another attempted to communicate with a group of men at a table with about a dozen empty beer glasses on it. The two detectives approached the counter.

"Evening officer," said Rizzo to the young cop, flashing his badge to him. The young man looked immediately relieved. "What's the situation?"

The young officer frowned and said in an accusing way, "Well that's what I've been trying to find out, but the barman isn't being very cooperative." He shot the big apron-clad man behind the counter a fiery glance like a tattling boy.

"You've done good work, son. We'll take it from here. Why don't you see if you can get a statement from one of the patrons."

As the officer nodded dutifully and walked away, Rizzo turned his attention to the barkeep, a thick, baldheaded man with a big, red nose and a thin layer of stubble on his cheeks. "Evening. I'm Sergent Rizzo and this is my partner Detective Lawrence. The name outside says Grady's Pub. You Grady?"

The barkeep grunted a weak affirmation.

"I understand there was some kind of incident here tonight?"

The barkeep grunted once more, shrugged, and started washing a dirty glass.

"What happened exactly?"

"Nothing happened here," snapped Grady the barman.

"Then why did someone call and report it?"

The barkeep shrugged again and said, "I dunno. I didn't call no one. Now why don't you fellas just be on your way. You're disrupting my business."

Rizzo gritted his teeth in annoyance. He was sick and tired of having to deal with uncooperative people. It was bad enough to have to swim against the current in the river of corruption in the city, but it didn't make it any easier that the citizens he was trying to help were against him too.

"You see those lights out there?" said Rizzo pointing at the squad car outside. "Those are going to sit there, glowing and flashing right there parked outside your bar until you start talking."

The big man released a low growl. "Fine, yeah there was something. Just a little fight between two guys, and one guy took out a gun. I scared him off with my shotgun and that was the end of it."

"This was the robot?"

The barman looked slightly surprised by the mention of the android. "Naw the robot left a minute or two later."

"So the robot was not the one with the gun?"

"Nope."

Lawrence asked, "Who was the other guy then?"

The barkeep shrugged and said, "Dunno, he was wearing a black hood."

"What were they fighting about?" asked Rizzo.

The big man raised his shoulders up high and then let them drop. "The robot saw the guy tryin' to sneak out the front and he suddenly jumped at him."

"What can you tell us about this robot? Ever seen him before?"

"You ever seen a robot drink something before? Yeah, me neither. This is the first robot I've had in here. He was wearing a hat and coat and was asking questions like some kinda private eye."

"What did he want to know?"

"He was asking about a guy who came in here earlier."

"Who was it?" asked Rizzo, beginning to grow both excited and impatient. Finally he was getting somewhere, but he had to squeeze every drop of information out of the guy like an almost empty tube of toothpaste.

"I dunno. Some pretty boy with blonde hair and blue eyes. I didn't pay him much attention. Coulda been anyone."

"Could you ID him if you saw him again?"

Grady shrugged once more and pointed at Lawrence. "Could have even been this kid."

"Detective Lawrence has brown hair," said Rizzo in a flat tone.

"Like I said, it could have been anyone."

Rizzo leaned over the counter and grabbed the barkeep by the collar and pulled him towards him causing him to drop the glass he was polishing into the sink with a loud clank. "Now you listen here! It's late, I'm tired, and you're really starting to rub me the wrong way. If you don't shape up your act you can spend the night down at the station."

"Hey, police brutality!" exclaimed the barkeep. Lawrence, looking alarmed, placed a hand on Rizzo's shoulder, but looked uncertain what to say.

"You're welcome to file a complaint later," stated Rizzo firmly. "So what's it gonna be? You talk and we go our separate ways or you sit in a concrete box until you change your mind?"

"All right, all right," said the barkeep with his open hands up beside his head in a submissive posture. Rizzo let him go, shoving him gently away from him. The barkeep straightened his shirt, cursing, "Jeez, you damned coppers are worse than the cons. It's like I said though, he was just some young blonde guy. Came in here with an older woman and they left a little while before the robot came in. I don't know anything else."

"What about that girl?" commented a sleepy looking man on the drinkers' side of the counter. He hiccupped midway through his sentence.

"What girl?" asked Rizzo looking first at the speaker and then at the barkeep.

The barkeep, looking like his memory had just been revitalized, explained, "Yeah that's right, there was a girl with the robot. Pretty young thing who looked a bit like a mouse in a room full of cats."

"Did you catch a name?" asked Lawrence. The barkeep shook his head. "Can you describe her?"

"I just did. Pretty, young, timid. She had long, dark hair up in a bun. I don't know nothing else."

"Could you ID the girl if you saw her again?" asked Lawrence.

"Do you know how many people walk in here every night?" asked the barman.

Lawrence looked over each shoulder, scanning the room briefly. "About fifteen?"

"A comedian, eh? So are we finished here now or what?"

The two detectives stepped back out into the cold, biting air, rabid and vicious with icy winter teeth tearing into their unprotected faces. Rizzo dug his fists down into his puffy, navy blue coat, blowing out a gust of white mist with his annoyed sigh. Lawrence shivered and produced a "Brrr" sound.

Rizzo was in a sour mood. Somehow the encounter had left him with even more unanswered questions than before and had brought him no closer to his target. Rizzo had always been temperamental, but sometimes he had the feeling that the older he got the more impatient he became. The thrill of the hunt, the intrigue of the puzzle, the glory of bringing forth justice; somehow these were things that no longer appealed to him, but instead just left him tired and frustrated.

"If only we knew who that girl was who was with him," said Lawrence sounding a little bit down. "Right?"

Rizzo didn't respond. Instead he stared straight ahead, across the street from the pub. A bright yellow sign read "Straight Shooter", and down beneath it, just above the door, was a surveillance camera. Wordlessly, the sergeant crossed the street while his confused partner scurried after him with cold-stiffened limbs.

The older detective looked down at his watch. 9:05 and the lights were still on inside. He thought it was odd that a gun store would be open so late at night, but then again, these days guns seemed to be about as much an addition as drugs and alcohol, so he supposed the people had to get their fix any time of day. He pushed open the door which knocked against a series of bells dangling from the ceiling. Pretty low-tech even by Rizzo's standards.

The strangely yellowish lighting in the room and the faint buzzing emanating from somewhere up above conjured the image of bees. The walls were lined with rifles standing upright and alert. Beneath them were metal rods with handguns packaged in plastic hanging from them like action figures in a toy store. Behind a small counter sat a shifty-eyed man with a cigarette in his mouth and long hair in a ponytail. He had a prosthetic arm, not dissimilar from that of the android Rizzo was searching for. The cyborg glared at the newcomers, one eye squinted small and the other opened wide.

"Evening," said Rizzo, flashing his badge. "I'm Sergeant Rizzo and this is Detective Lawrence. Does your camera out front work?"

Still giving the evil eye, the one-armed man sat silently for a long moment before saying, "Yeah."

"Would you mind giving us a look at the footage from the last hour or two?"

"Yeah."

"Yeah you'll show us?"

"No. Yeah, I mind."

Rizzo sighed loudly, and it came out halfway as a growl. "We're just trying to investigate a fight that went on across the street."

"You thugs got a warrant?"

The older detective ran his hand over his face, stroking his thick mustache. He would have liked to tear off the man's mechanical arm and beat him over the head with it. He took a deep breath to calm himself. "You know, I'm thinking we ought to have a closer look at your dealer's license. What do you think, Jim?"

Lawrence, nodded and said, "Yeah, this place seems pretty suspect."

"Hey my papers are all in order, man," protested the store owner.

"Sure, they are," said Rizzo. "But just to be on the safe I think I'll call up the ATF and have them double-check it. They should take a look at your books too and make sure you properly documented the Firearm Owner's ID Cards for all your sales. I'm sure you've kept those records from the last ten years, so you've got nothing to worry about."

"Hey man, not cool. This is like…bullying or something."

"And you know what? While we're opening up your books anyway why don't we also just call up the IRS and make sure all your bills are in order?"

"Okay, okay," said the man, putting up both hands in front of him as if trying to stop the force of the detective's words with them. "Lock the door and flip the sign, will ya?"

Lawrence turned around and stared at the door for a moment in a confused fashion wondering what he was supposed to do until he saw the little metal knob beneath the handle. After rotating it and producing a faint metallic clank, he grabbed a paper sign that read "closed" and flipped it around to face the street, causing it to read "open" to those inside. When the young detective finished this notably analog task, he turned back around, his eyes looking like those of a man who had just visited a warzone.

The store owner stood up and went into the back room while the two detectives cautiously followed. An ancient computer sat on a desk in the corner of the dark room with an LCD monitor which miraculously still worked, although with a few missing pixels here and there. The gun seller sat down on a dirty plastic chair in front of the desk and took hold of a mouse which had once been a solid grey but now had dark stains from human grease on each of the two buttons. After a few clicks he sat back so the detectives could see the video playing on the screen.

"What's the timestamp there?" asked Rizzo.

"Eight. You said an hour ago, right?"

"Go back a little further, maybe another hour."

The video was set back to seven and then played forward at double speed for a few minutes until Rizzo suddenly said, "There! Stop," pointing at the screen.

"That looks like the robot going inside," said Lawrence. "I can't see any faces though."

Rizzo wrote down the timestamp in his little notebook and gestured for the man to resume the playback. After a few moments, or about fifteen in terms of the timestamps, Lawrence excitedly exclaimed, "There!"

Rizzo leaned in close and said, "That must be the guy the barkeep mentioned with the hood on. Why would a person be coming out of a bar wearing a black mask? Could you continue from here at normal speed?" The masked man stumbled out of the pub, nearly tripping as he narrowly avoided running into a pedestrian. He quickly hailed a passing taxi and jumped inside. "Could you stop it again?" Rizzo wrote down the plate numbers and then said, "Okay, continue."

Just after the vehicle was out of sight, the robot emerged from the bar, standing tall and alert, looking in every direction for signs of the masked man. Behind it stood a shy girl, cowering.

"No way," commented Lawrence in amazement. "Isn't that Sophie Harper? The girl who found the body."

Rizzo leaned in close and strained his eyes to make something out of the poor resolution of the screen. "I think you're right." The robot took a few steps forward, turned to face the girl, and a moment later the two of them hurried away, exiting the view of the camera.

"But what is she doing with the robot?" asked Lawrence rhetorically.

"Why don't we go ask her that ourselves," suggested Rizzo.

CHAPTER 19

The girl paced the living room nervously, chewing on a fingernail with her elbow cradled in her other hand. While she attempted to wear a trench into the carpet with her repetitive motion, Seven sat calmly on the sofa with the leather bag the masked man had dropped placed neatly on his lap.

With careful, deliberate motion from perfectly steady hands, the android unlatched the satchel and threw the flap open. The detective began to examine the contents of the bag, starting with the smallest and foremost pockets. He found a bundle of business cards with the name Ethan Willis printed on them, a credit card with Speculo printed beneath Willis's name, a lanyard with an RFID chip attached to it, and a modern vintage-style ticket to a boxing match next week with the faces of the main event fighters floating in 3D above the card. In the next pocket the detective found a pair of high-end headphones and a purple t-shirt with a picture of a green army tank with a pink brain sitting above the main gun and the text "Chicago Think Tank" floating above it in colorful bubble-letters. Finally, in the largest pocket, Seven found the computer which Willis had shown him during their first encounter.

"Shouldn't we maybe call the police?" whined Sophie.

"No police."

"Oh god, what have I gotten myself into?" the girl asked herself.

"You're fine," Seven reassured her. "By the way, did that guy look familiar to you? The masked man."

She halted her pacing and stared at him, her wide, teary eyes sweating a cocktail of tears spiced with fear and shock. "Wha- what do you mean?"

"That was the same guy who shot at me in that alley two days ago."

"Oh, right. Yeah, it did look like him." Sophie hesitated, biting her lip, before saying, "Are you sure we shouldn't call someone? The police? Or what about your owner. Wouldn't he know what to do?"

"I've got it under control, but I'm sure he'd be flattered to know that pretty little things like you are constantly asking for him."

Despite the girl's feverish anxiety, she blushed at the android's comment, then meekly asked, "What are you going to do?"

"I'm going to solve the case I was originally hired to investigate," Seven replied simply, and refused to give any further comment after that. When it became apparent that the conversation was over, the girl resumed her nervous wanderings.

The detective withdrew the computer from the pouch with the same care with which one would handle a newborn baby and set the bag to the side. He inspected the object peripherally and then, ignoring the soft, nervous moans from the pacing girl, he activated the device and plugged himself into it. Seven began by scanning the machine in the same way he had done originally, and after finding nothing new, he initiated a deeper, more intensive scan. After he sat in perfect stillness for nearly half an hour, Sophie grew impatient and disappeared into the kitchen. When the detective's search had completed and failed to produce any new information, the android frowned with his jaw slightly to one side in the same way Vic always did when he was puzzled.

Seven's next approach was to examine the malware itself for clues in the hopes that he might find something like a digital fingerprint to help him learn where this piece of software had originated. After decompiling the executable, Seven examined the code in the hopes of finding something which might uniquely identify the program's creator. The process of compilation is irreversible, so the sources that Seven was examining were only approximations with most of the original data missing, however he did manage to find a few text strings that stood out to him including: "Please don't modify this executable...Changes may damage your operating system", "irc.ip-info.xyz:6697", "#controlroom", and "/tmp/cache/64/regnabdaeh/".

Seven wondered briefly if the hacker had been using internet relay chat, an almost prehistoric method of communication, to issue remote commands to the rootkit. The android allowed himself to idly wonder for only a microsecond before attempting to find out for himself. He connected to the server and channel he had discovered but found only an empty chat room, nor could he find any evidence of any other channels on the server or other users connected.

Although he was sure he had yet to blow his case wide-open, Seven was nevertheless satisfied that his investigation had yielded fruit, and he was convinced that he had found a valuable clue. He shelved his new findings for the time being and proceeded to peruse Willis's emails.

While reading a mildly interesting discussion between the man and Grayson from a week before, motion from somewhere behind him caught his attention on the reflective surface of the tablet. Seven dropped the computer and dove to the floor just as a metal baseball bat came hurdling in a downward arc towards where the detective's head had been just milliseconds before, colliding with the white leather cushions of the couch instead.

With a surprising level of agility, the android propped himself up and spun around to confront the would-be homerun hitter. Seven ducked just in time to avoid a sideswipe to the face, and, utilizing the springing force provided by his crouch, he bounded towards the masked man who was still recovering from his wide swing. Seven grabbed the man by the face as if it were a piece of fruit and squeezed hard while pushing the man towards the wall.

Sophie screamed, having been lured back into the living room by the ruckus. The masked man lashed out at Seven with his bat, striking him in the side weakly with the limited space he had to wind up his swing. After a series of ineffective blows, the man threw his weapon to the side and withdrew his pistol from his coat pocket. With his free hand, Seven grabbed the gloved hand holding the pistol and pointed it away.

The doorbell rang in the background, momentarily causing the two organics in the room to freeze in surprise while Seven utilized the distraction to try to crush his attacker's fingers which were tightly clutching the grip of the deadly handheld tool. The masked man let out a cry of pain and ceased to resist the hold the metal spider had upon his face. Instead, he began to focus the strength of both arms on his weapon, slowly pulling the barrel closer to Seven's torso. The bell tolled once again, and like a prize fighter reacting to familiar stimuli, the masked man pulled the trigger, missing the detective by only a centimeter.

Calculating that his risk of receiving grievous damage was growing higher by the second, the android threw his opponent to the side and backed away. At the same time the front door of the house exploded inward, slamming into the wall with a violent crash, the wooden frame splintering and spraying sharp little toothpicks everywhere. Two men entered with guns held out in front of them, both with grim, serious expressions on their tired faces.

"Police!" shouted the younger man who had entered first. "Nobody move!"

The older man Seven recognized as the police sergeant who had questioned him at the station. With laser precision, the man focused his bloodshot eyes on the android, his moustache quivering with excitement. He didn't even seem to register that there was anyone else present in the room. Despite their tired redness, Rizzo's eyes had a glint in them, like the look a cat has when it's about to pounce. It was the wild, hungry look of a hunter with his prey in the crosshairs.

The masked man, still lying on the carpet, panicked and began to fire at random with his gun pointed in the direction of the newcomers. The young cop screamed, a pathetic high-pitched wail, and his hand rose to grasp his left shoulder as he slumped against the wall.

Time froze while the android processed all the variables and considered every possible course of action. He looked at the hitman with his gun still poised to fire. He saw Sophie cowering in fear in the corner of the room with her head between her knees. He saw the young cop sliding down to the floor with his back to the wall, leaving a red streak along the way down. He saw Rizzo suddenly realizing that Seven was not the most immediate danger in the room as he looked down at his injured partner in horror. By Seven's calculations, his odds were best if he disappeared from the house while the three gunmen were distracted by one-another. Something inside of him, however, somehow prevented him from simply slipping out the back despite the cold logic of his circuitry suggesting it. He saw a relatively high probability that the masked man would continue firing and would likely strike flesh once more since the two officers were packed in a narrow hallway, and Rizzo still didn't seem to have noticed the shooter.

Finally, Seven made what he calculated to be the most optimal decision. He sped towards the front door, crouched low to make himself a smaller target, and he tackled Rizzo who was still staring dumbly at his partner. The two crashed hard on the floor just as the hitman fired twice more, bullets flying by overhead and burrowing into their new homes in the wall.

Seven heard the impotent click of the gun's empty barrel behind him and stood back up before the shooter had the chance to reload.

Without a moment's hesitation, the detective ran through the open door and out into the street, never looking back. Seven continued to run with remarkable speed considering his weight, his metal feet clanking noisily against the pavement and echoing in the silent, suburban night.

The evening's fights and the long run had been a considerable drain on his battery, and he would need to find a place to charge, but he was still quite satisfied with the day. He was making progress.

CHAPTER 20

An ambulance pulled out in front of the house about twenty minutes after Rizzo's call. Two white plastic-plated androids with red crosses on their chests stepped out the back of the boxy vehicle carrying a gurney. They were followed by a young medical technician carrying a black plastic suitcase.

"It's about damned time you guys got here," cursed Rizzo, one hand squeezing the other nervously, as he watched their approach from the porch. "He's inside."

Rizzo led them into the hallway where his partner sat slumped against the wall with a white, bloodied towel pressed to his wound. The young technician crouched beside Lawrence and opened his suitcase full of equipment. He slipped his hands into squeaky gloves, picked up a pair of scissors, and cut open the detective's shirt to examine his wound while one of the robots fastened a thin metal bracer around Lawrence's forearm.

"92 over 66 with a heart rate of 71 bpm," stated the android after activating the display on the diagnostic bracelet.

"That's a good sign," stated the young paramedic, picking up a small device that looked a bit like a hot glue gun and spraying a sort of yellowish gel into the wound which hardened almost instantly.

"He'll be all right?" asked Rizzo nervously.

"What are you talking about, I've never been better," laughed Lawrence weakly with a thin smile on his pallid face, wincing from the motion his chest made.

"I don't want to make any promises," said the technician, "but yeah, it doesn't look too bad. I've seen worse."

In a soothing voice, the android which had until now stood idle stated, "The projected mortality rate for such an injury is—"

"Nobody wants to hear that!" said the paramedic harshly before the robot could finish. "Sorry about that. This one is new."

The two androids carefully assisted Lawrence onto the gurney and the technician attached an IV to it and plugged it into the diagnostic armband. The robots then proceeded to roll the wounded detective back outside to their vehicle. Rizzo walked alongside the gurney looking defeated.

"I'm sorry, Jim," said the older detective. "It's my fault. I should have seen it sooner. I reacted too slowly."

"Nonsense," said Lawrence.

"No, really. I was so damned fixated on that stupid robot that I didn't even see the gunman until it was too late. And then the robot knocked me down and by the time I was back on my feet the other guy had slipped out back."

"You'll get him, Toni. And when you find that masked lunatic you rough him up a bit for me, will ya?"

Rizzo nodded and then watched as his partner was loaded into the back of the ambulance. He stood there on the sidewalk leading from the house to the street, staring unseeingly into the direction of the vehicle's departure for a few minutes, lost in thought. He absentmindedly brought his hand to the back of his head to touch the sore little mountain that was already forming where he had hit his head on the floor after the robot had jumped him.

That tackle had likely saved his life. Had that been the robot's intent? Or had it simply been trying to escape and Rizzo had been in the way? And if it had been intentional, had it been an act of free will or was it an imperative of the machine's programming? Rizzo wasn't sure what to believe, but at this point he was convinced that the robot, human or not, was a being that did what it wanted. Its behavior was too unusual, and yet simultaneously familiar, to simply be the result of programming. That was his expert opinion as a man who had to ask his nine-year-old daughter to help him sync his calendar to his phone, and he was going to stick with it until proven otherwise.

He shook his head to knock the thoughts away and turned around to head back into the house. The detective had already summoned a forensics team, however they had yet to arrive, so he would take the opportunity to investigate before they started tromping around contaminating the crime scene.

The frame of front door of the house was destroyed from when he had kicked it open, but the door itself seemed undamaged, and the lock appeared functional. He found five bullet holes in the wall of the foyer, and notably one of them was at exactly the height of his head. There was a long bloody streak about a meter long on the other side of the hallway. Inside the house the detective found Sophie still sitting on the floor with her head between her knees, alternating between sobs and heavy, controlled breathing like she was in the process of giving birth. The sliding glass door in the back of the house was open, and there were no signs of damage. The detective discovered a sixth bullet hole in one of the leather cushions of the sofa. Upon the sofa sat a leather satchel and a computer. On the floor in front of the couch was a metal baseball bat.

Rizzo approached the crying girl, who had calmed herself slightly, and said, "Miss Harper?" The girl flinched without looking up and drew her arms tighter around her knees. "Miss Harper, look at me."

Slowly, reluctantly, she looked up at him, stopping when her eyes reached his chest.

"You're okay," said Rizzo gently. "They're gone now. It's just you and me, and soon a few more guys from the department will be here. No one is going to hurt you. Understand?"

She opened her mouth slightly and then closed it again and sucked on her lower lip, then she bobbed her head in a wide, slow up and down motion.

"Why don't you have a seat up here on the couch," suggested Rizzo, not wanting to crouch down on the floor because of his bad knees, and not wanting to continue staring down because his neck was sore from the whiplash of being tackled. He offered a hand to help her up.

Sophie stared at it dumbly for a moment before finally extending her own hand and standing up. She walked over to the couch and sat down, staring at the coffee table in front of her.

"Miss Harper, what exactly happened here?"

"I-I don't really know," she replied so quietly he had to lean forward to hear it.

"What do you mean? You were here, weren't you?"

"I was in the other room, and then I heard noises and came back and…it all happened so fast."

"All right," said Rizzo patiently wiping his hand over his muzzle as he often did when he was frustrated. "Then why don't you start from the beginning. How did it happen that you were in West Engelwood with the robot earlier tonight?"

She looked him in the eye for the first time, surprise all over her face. After a few seconds she recovered and her gaze drifted back downwards. "He…he came here wanting to use my access to Orion's network to…" She paused for a moment, perhaps thinking how best to continue. "He wanted to look for a virus or something. He didn't really say. He was looking for that computer." She gestured with her head towards the tablet lying on the couch beside her. "He said he tracked it down to West Engelwood and then asked me to come with him."

"And you went?" asked the detective, incredulous.

"I…I guess I was curious, and somehow he distracted me from feeling bad…you know, about this whole thing. So much for that though. Now it's even worse."

Rizzo gave her a stern look which Sophie did not see with her downcast eyes. "You understand that the robot is a murder suspect, don't you? You were aiding and abetting a wanted criminal."

Sophie's lower lip quivered and she looked like she might start bawling at any moment. "I…Oh god. Am I going to jail?"

Rizzo tilted his head upwards, despite the soreness in his neck to look in the direction of heaven, silently cursing whatever deity that was deriving pleasure from the trial of patience he was forced to endure. The detective sighed loudly and said, "Okay, and what happened when you got there?"

"We went into a bar because Seven was looking for Ethan."

"Ethan? Ethan Willis?" Rizzo pulled his little notebook and pen out of his coat pocket.

"Yes, that's right. Seven was looking for Mr. Willis," narrated the girl, fingering the bullet hole in the couch beside her. "He talked to the bartender for a while, but he said Mr. Willis already left, and then Seven got into a fight with the masked man."

"This was the same masked man who was here in your house?"

"I guess so."

"And what happened after you left the bar?"

"We came back here and Seven was looking at the computer for a really long time. I don't know what he was doing with it. And then everything got crazy."

"Why did this masked man come here? How did he know to come here? Were you followed?"

"I don't know."

Rizzo frowned and ran his thumb and forefinger over his moustache. "How did he get into the house?"

"I-I don't know. I guess the back door must have been unlocked."

Rizzo sighed and turned his back to the girl. A rectangle of brilliant colors hanging from the wall caught his attention and he stepped towards it. The painting had a strange depth to it as if he was staring through a window into another dimension, and the longer he stared at it, the more he had the impression that it was slowly moving. He blinked uncomfortably, feeling somewhat disoriented, yet fascinated.

"You like it?" asked Sophie shyly.

"Huh?" Rizzo broke his gaze and turned back to face the girl. "I guess so. A little bit modern for my tastes, but it's interesting. Who made it?"

"I did," she said proudly, momentarily looking calm and collected, and then her face filled with guilt for having felt good when she should be feeling bad.

"Really?"

"Yeah. I started out studying graphic design at university, but when I found out the field was completely saturated and there were no career prospects I switched to business. And look where that got me." She looked around the room and her eyes came to rest on the bloodstain on the wall behind where she sat.

"You look like you're doing pretty well for yourself if you ask me," replied the detective a little jealously. The young woman's house was nearly twice the size of his own, and in a much better neighborhood.

The room was silent for a few minutes after that. Shyly, with her face a bright pink, Sophie asked, "Do...do you think it's possible that the masked man worked for Mr. Grayson?"

Rizzo ruffled his brow, irritated by the unexpected question. "What makes you say that?"

"Well," said the girl who then hesitated before continuing. "On the day that Mr. Grayson was m-murdered, I was walking with Seven outside while he asked me some questions, and while we were out he was attacked by a masked man who looked just like the one tonight."

"This was before the murder?" asked Rizzo, excitement spilling into his voice. He clenched his little notebook tighter, bending it slightly.

"Yes, and he dropped a note with Seven's name on it and beneath it were Mr. Grayson's initials."

"Why didn't you mention this when we interviewed you after you found Grayson's body?" asked Rizzo a bit too harshly, causing Sophie to flinch.

"I thought you already knew. Seven called the police and gave a report to the officer."

Rizzo ran his hand over his face once again, and then made a note to search for this police report to verify her story.

Timidly, Sophie asked, "Do you think it's possible that the masked man worked for Mr. Grayson? And...and after he failed to kill Seven, Seven killed Mr. Grayson in retaliation?"

Rizzo hadn't been thinking it before, but he was certainly considering that possibility now.

CHAPTER 21

Seven spent the night charging in the library of John Morris University just outside of downtown Chicago. The building was open 24 hours and provided induction panels for the students to charge their devices. There were a few students cramming for exams, and two extremely tired looking student workers at the front desk, but nobody paid the robot any attention.

The next morning he summoned a cab to bring him to Lincoln Park. The detective stepped outside to find himself facing an intricate wrought iron fence, each spindle rising up to form a sharp little spear that said 'admire me from afar'. Behind the fence were short rows of well-trimmed hedges and the remnants of recently departed flowerbeds. This fine garden spanned 15 meters until it reached an extravagant, three-storey mansion constructed with huge, white stone bricks. The central component of the house rose in a gentle slope to form a crest with an obtuse angle. The two wings on to the left and right of the center stood slightly shorter and slightly further back.

Seven walked along the sidewalk until he reached the gate which was locked. He rang the bell and waited. To the android's surprise, a moment later, the gate opened without anyone asking him to identify himself. Seven continued up the path to the cherry wood door which opened as soon as he reached it.

A bulky android which someone had dressed up in a tuxedo glared at him through the doorway. A robot with a bowtie was a rather ridiculous sight, and the irony of this judgment was not lost on Seven who looked down briefly at his own attire. The fancy mechanical man displayed an expression as near to disgust as imaginable for a metal face.

"Oh," said the butler in a tinny, snobbish voice. "I was expecting one of Mrs. Grayson's solicitors."

"Sorry to disappoint," said Seven, wondering what kind of self-respecting butler would open the door without checking the camera first.

As if he had intercepted the detective's thought stream, the butler stated, "The camera and intercom at the gate are currently out of order. I don't suppose you're the repairman?"

"Another disappointment. I'm on a roll today. I'm here to see Elizabeth Grayson. Is she in?"

"Do you have an appointment?"

"That depends."

The butler cocked his thick head curiously and asked, "On what?"

"Well apparently whether or not she's in depends on whether or not I have an appointment, so we might as well say that whether or not I have an appointment depends on whether or not she's in."

The butler stared at Seven silently for a moment, contemplating this circular dependency. His head, still tilted to one side, slowly drifted its gaze down towards the welcome mat beneath the detective's feet. Seven wondered if perhaps he had gone too far and broken the poor creature. If it was that easy then someone deserved to be fired.

A derisive cackle erupted from somewhere inside the house, and a woman who looked only slightly less artificial than the butler stepped into view. She had her blonde hair up in a bun with a pair of Asian eating utensils stuck inside of it, and she was wearing a short, pink silk robe with no indication that there was anything underneath.

"You've confused the poor thing," she said with a maliciously playful smile on her bloated lips. She turned her back to them, but then looked over her shoulder seductively and said, "Well, come on then."

The butler bot stepped aside to allow Seven to enter, and then closed the door behind him. Seven followed the pink lady through the lavishly furnished house until they reached a glass winter garden attached to the back of the mansion. The room was filled with lush, green palm trees and tropical flowers. Seven counted 57 different species of orchid just within his current line of sight. The room was so humid that he wondered if perhaps it had shorted some of the butler's circuitry.

The woman sat down in a wicker chair with a thick pillow on it and crossed her legs in a wide, exaggerated motion which probably would have thrown a human man off guard. She stared at the detective with an expression of amusement for a moment before revealing, "I know who you are." She spoke as if she had seen right through the detective's clever disguise.

"Is that so? Who am I then?"

"You're the robot they were talking about on the news. The one that the police think murdered my husband."

"If you know who I am then why haven't you called the police?"

Her mouth curled into a devilish grin which threatened to burst her lips. "What makes you think I didn't already?"

"You were obviously close enough to overhear my conversation with your butler, and I didn't hear you speaking on the phone in the background. Plus the entire conversation lasted 42 seconds, 61 if you include the time it took for the gate to open and for me to reach the front door. Hardly enough time to explain yourself to the police. And besides, based on their track record, even if you did call them I have about half an hour until they get here. More than enough time to have a conversation and for me to be on my way."

The woman threw back her head and uttered the syllable, "Hah!" in a loud staccato. "I like you."

She looked at Seven thoughtfully and said, "No, I didn't call the police. Either you're innocent, or you did me a favor. I'm about to inherit quite a lot of money." She uttered her last sentence with the restrained giddiness of businesswoman who just closed a major deal.

"Well," said Seven, "sorry to break it to you Mrs. Grayson, but I did not kill your husband. That's actually why I'm here. I was hoping to get some more insights into his life to find out who really did him in so I can clear my name."

"You want to know who might have had motive to kill Miles?" asked the plastic lady with amusement in her eyes. "It would be easier to list the people who didn't want the man dead. His lawyer for one," she held up a closed fist and then extended her index finger. "Miles was putting that man's kids through college." She stared down at the lonesome digit and then shrugged, and said, "Hm, I suppose that's all really."

"I understand you were in the process of divorce. Is that right?"

"That's right."

"May I ask why?"

"Why not, it's no secret. Everyone in the state knows by now about Miles and his difficulties keeping it in his pants. Hah! Half the state has probably personally been inside his pants at this point. I happen to know for a fact that he was banging at least three women at his workplace, right inside his office. Miles was always a slut, but as long as he was subtle about it and didn't defecate where he ate I could look the other way. The platinum credit card helped too I suppose.

"But then last spring I caught him here in our very own bed with the maid. Do you want to know what he said to me when I walked in and found him there on his back with that skinny little bimbo bouncing on top of him? He said, 'Oh, hi Beth. Could you give us a few minutes?'" For a moment the playful vigor in her eyes faded and her voice faltered slightly. "Can you believe that?"

"I guess you could say karma is a bitch," said Seven, watching closely for a reaction. As he spoke he wondered why the Graysons would hire a human maid in this day and age. He had the strong suspicion that it had been the mister's idea.

The seductive succubus smile returned to her lips once more. "You could say that. The only thing that really makes me sad about his death now is that I'll never get to tell him I was plowing that thick stallion who trims our hedges." She threw back her head and laughed. When she quieted she had a gleam in her grinning eyes. It was the expression of a prisoner freshly relieved of her shackles.

"So let me get this straight," said Seven. "You wanted to divorce the guy because he was having a little something on the side even though you were too?" The android was thoroughly convinced that humans would forever be an enigma to him. They were a puzzle that he wasn't certain he ever really wanted to solve, although he had to admit they kept things interesting.

"Well, not as far as his divorce attorney knew," she laughed. "And it looks like I won't be needing to pay mine anymore now."

While the woman laughed, relishing in her newfound freedom, Seven waited, stone-faced, for her grim satisfaction to subside. Before he had a chance to speak however, she said, "I can see the question burning on your tongue. I can read you like a book; a man is a man, metal or flesh. Well go on then, ask."

The detective accepted the invitation and asked the question which had been on his mind since the moment he arrived, "Did you kill your husband?"

"No," she replied simply, head held high with a proud expression. "Although, I almost wish I had after that humiliation he caused me when he froze my account."

"I want to be perfectly clear, so allow me to rephrase. Are you responsible for the death of Miles Grayson?"

She looked at him curiously, trying as hard as she could to form a wrinkle on her botoxed brow and coming up short. "You think I hired someone?"

"It's a possibility I have to consider."

"With what money? Like I said, he froze my account."

"You've got a lot of nice stuff in here. Jewelry, paintings, maybe a few antiques. I'm sure you could pull something together if you were determined."

"Yes, I'm sure I could, but I didn't."

"All right. Where were you on Tuesday night?"

"I was here at home with Jenkins."

"Jenkins?"

"The butler. I believe you've met."

Seven was sure he could verify her alibi if he checked the butler's logs, but it would be a pointless effort. The statement of a robot was weak. All he had to do was look at his own case; the secretary at the Orion Center had been manipulated to completely forget him. For now, Seven would accept the woman's statement and see if there was anything else of value she could tell him. She watched him thoughtfully, wondering what he would do next.

"Fine," said Seven, brushing off her disinterest in defending herself. "How about last night?"

"You want to know where I was last night?" The woman sounded surprised. "I was in a part of town which looked like a warzone letting a much poorer man than me buy me drinks."

"This man got a name?"

She looked puzzled and hesitated for a moment before closing her eyes lightly and breathing in deep, her head doing a tiny dance as she exhaled. "Willis was his name, though I'm not sure why that should matter. He was in the process of trying to negotiate a deal with my husband, rather unsuccessfully I might add. Now that Miles is gone I'm about to become one of the majority shareholders, so Willis invited me for drinks to try to get on my good side."

"What did you talk about?"

"Honestly I don't know why you're so fixated on him." The unspoken conclusion of that sentence was 'when you have me here to talk about'. "He just rambled on about his overly complicated business idea and some babble about elements."

"Did he have anything with him? A bag or a computer?"

"I have no idea. I was more concerned with protecting my own handbag in a place like that."

"Did you happen to come across a man wearing a black balaclava?"

"What kind of absurd question is that?"

"All right, fine," concluded the android, changing the subject before he lost the woman's cooperation. "You suggested that a lot of people would have had motive to kill your husband. Got any names that stand out?"

"No, not particularly. I suppose there was that IT guy who punched him. Now that was sweet! Oh the laughs that brought me. My last happy memory of Miles I suppose."

"Do you know anything about the incident?"

Elizabeth Grayson swiped a paw in the detective's direction to deflect his words. "I don't know anything about that. As I understand it, Miles was looking for a good reason to fire the man—something with a K...Karovski maybe—without making him into a martyr. He was apparently quite the troublemaker, and Miles suspected him of being behind a number of incidents—minor data breaches, something called 'defacement', blah blah blah. In the end he pinned some piracy thing on the man I think."

Seven's expression betrayed nothing, however internally he raised an eyebrow. The woman had claimed to know nothing, and yet she had told him more than anyone else had so far. "Did your husband talk about his work often?"

"No, never."

"You seem to know quite a bit about it."

Mrs. Grayson smiled menacingly. "I have my ways."

"Sure. Besides the IT guy, anything else come to mind?"

The woman seemed to truly consider for a few minutes, her forefinger idly bouncing up and down on her lower lip like it was a trampoline. "Well...he did like to gamble now and then."

"What was his poison?"

"There's a gentlemen's club by the harbor where he sometimes went. I've never been there, but I understand they played poker usually. He also sometimes went to the race track or the Coliseum to bet on a match."

"I see. Anything else you can tell me?" She slowly turned her head left and then right without breaking eye-contact. "All right, then I thank you for your cooperation. You've been very helpful Mrs. Grayson."

"Please, call me Beth."

"Sure."

"Are you sure you won't stay a little longer?" Suddenly in that moment she looked small and old and lonely with a hint of pleading bleeding into her voice.

"Sorry, but I've got another appointment. Maybe I'll be back."

CHAPTER 22

Fuller Park looked about as appealing as a used handkerchief, but the kids playing in the streets didn't seem bothered by it. Seven's car had a hard time maneuvering around them when he pulled up just before noon. He stepped out of the vehicle, ignoring an advertisement for some new miracle drug which only occasionally had fatal side-effects.

The detective glanced at the dirty, decrepit apartment building. Apparently he had liked the place so much he decided to make a repeat performance. As he had the previous two visits, he slipped through the poor security door outside and treaded down the filthy carpeted hallway until he reached the dwelling of Max Kaminski. He knocked.

The door opened, this time without unnecessary violence, and pale face showed itself through the crack. "Aw, man, not you again," said the face.

"Nice to see you too, pal," said Seven. "Let me in. We need to have a little chat, Maxi."

"No way, I saw the news. You're the one who killed Grayson. I should call the cops."

"Sure, that's one option. But if you did that I'd have to tell them about life and works of headbanger46. Maybe I'd direct them to a certain IRC server here or some piece of malware there. And if they going to show up at your place I suppose you'd need to pull out your shredder for your hard drives. Sounds like a pretty fun way to spend your afternoon, I guess."

Kaminski hesitated for a moment, clutching the door tightly with one white-knuckled hand while the other hand squeezed the knob from inside. Finally, he groaned and said, "Fine, get in!" He pulled open the door angrily and Seven entered the tiny apartment.

There was a wet towel lying in the middle of the room in a sad little pile, and there was a musty humidity in the air which made the mold on the ceiling moan with satisfaction. The man had apparently showered, probably for the first time in a while. His hair was still wet, and it clumped into thick cords making his head look like a nest of little black mouse tails. He was wearing black slacks and a white polo shirt which was wrinkled.

"Wow," said Seven dryly. "And here I was thinking you didn't own any pants."

Kaminski glowered. "I have a job interview. And I have to leave in about 25 minutes or else I'll be late."

"Decided to give up on online gaming stardom?"

In an annoyed tone spoken as if in mockery, Kaminski explained, "Apparently my landlord insists on seeing my new contract whenever I change jobs, and apparently streaming doesn't qualify in her eyes."

"And I suppose hacking doesn't either?" asked Seven watching carefully for a reaction.

"What do you want?"

"I want to know a little more about your relationship with Grayson. I don't think you were completely honest with me before."

"I already told you everything, man."

"A little bird brought me a rumor about defacements and data breaches. Got anything to say about that?"

"No, I don't."

"Let me rephrase. You clearly had a long and negative history with the upper management of Orion Industries. Then just about a week ago Grayson finally finds something he can use to sack you without looking bad, and when he does it you lash out at him and he has to call security. And just a few days after that he turns up dead with the camera feeds manipulated and secretary's memory wiped, and everyone thinks some dumb robot was behind it. Sounds like a pretty neat job. Got anything to say to that?"

"I've got an alibi, man, remember?"

"Sure, and I guess next you'll try to convince me that a man of your talents couldn't have manufactured a digital alibi like that."

Kaminski took a half step backwards and shifted his weight back and forth a few times in a rhythm out of sync with the shifting his eyes were doing.

"Level with me, Max. Did you kill Miles Grayson?"

"No!" Max shouted furiously, his face turning red. A thick vein bulged on his neck just above his collar.

"Maxi," said Seven like a disappointed father. "The only reason I was even at the Orion Center on Tuesday was because of a piece of malware that you wrote. Enough games."

The programmer's eyes widened in horror and confusion like a doe staring down the headlights of a tugboat. "Wha-what malware?"

"A little rootkit which transmits data to its friendlier twin on some remote system. The rootkit also takes instructions issued over an IRC channel."

"I-I don't know anything about that." Kaminski looked up at the blue spores on the ceiling for help.

"Pretty strange then that I found your name on it. It was apparently storing data in a directory called slash temp slash cache slash 64 slash regnabdaeh." The final word the detective pronounced as reg-nab-day. "Those last two directories backwards spell headbanger46. Your hiding places are about as clever as a 6-year-old."

Kaminski groaned and buried his face in his hands while he walked in a little circle around the room. He either didn't notice or didn't care that he was walking on top of his clothing which covered the floor.

The programmer let his hands drop like little wrecking balls, hitting his thighs, and said, "Look, yes I wrote that program, but I never used it. I just wrote it for fun."

"Well it was certainly fun for my client. How'd it end up loose in the wild? And how do you explain that it was transmitting to that very dev server you mentioned to me in our last conversation?"

"I have no idea how it ended up there. I gave it to someone I met online about a month ago." Kaminski's cheeks turned slightly pink, and Seven detected signs that the man's heart rate increased slightly.

"Who did you give it to?"

"A girl." That vein on his neck bulged again, and Seven could see the throbbing of his pulse. "I met her in a hacker chan on IRC and we sorta hit it off. She was interested in learning."

"And how did that lead to you giving her illegal software with self-incriminating filepaths?"

"I guess I kinda wanted to brag a little. You know, I wanted to look cool in front of her, so I showed her what I could do."

"Uh huh. And how do you know she was even a girl?" Seven knew the man wouldn't like the question, but the internet, and IRC in particular, was a place where the men were greasy-haired kids living in their parents' basements, and the women were middle-aged men who enjoyed getting attention.

"She told me," said Kaminski as if that would be some kind of incontrovertible evidence.

"Sure she did. Try again."

"Her nick was BlackAlice and she talked like a girl. Why would she lie? And what difference does it even make?"

"Fine. You managed to find the one girl on IRC. So you gave her this bug, and apparently she used it. How did it end up on your former dev server and how did it end up in my office the very same day of the murder?"

"I don't know man. I just gave it to her to show off and that was it. We didn't talk about it again."

"You got any chat logs from these conversations?"

Kaminski looked at the detective like he had just asked him for his credit card pin. "No way, man. You don't log on an SSL server. That's just not cool."

"Right. Show me the logs."

Kaminski stared at him for a long time before roaring in annoyance and stomping over to his desk. When he sat down the holographic display turned itself on, and he made a few hand gestures at it until he had conjured up a list of text files named with dates followed by the name of a channel or user. He opened a few, skimmed through the content and then flicked them away. At one point he practically punched one of the documents off the screen, and then turned his red face to see if the android had noticed anything. Seven of course noticed everything, but it wasn't as interesting as the programmer seemed to think. Finally, Kaminski located the conversation he was searching for and he rolled to the side so Seven had a clearer view.

It was a lot of very mediocre flirtation from the programmer's side and a lot of very obvious invitations to continue from the other. The conversation consisted of slightly more substance than a politician's promises. The only thing Seven was able to learn from these logs was that Kaminski did indeed share his homemade rootkit with another person along with instructions how to use it.

Kaminski sat in his leather desk chair which made croaking noises like a sick frog. He stared at the detective, searching for some sign that he was off the hook now. Seven's expressionless face left the man's soul malnourished.

Seven asked, "Did this girl ever mention a guy called Ethan Willis?"

Kaminski ruffled his brow and a little wrinkle grew out of the corner of each eye. "No, why? Should that name mean something to me?"

"You haven't heard the name Willis? Or Speculo?"

He jutted his chin out and tried to roll his eyes back to look at his brain. "Uh, no? Why?"

"Never mind. How do you think the receiving part ended up on this dev server at Orion?"

"There are plenty of ways you could get access to that server. Every developer has their own home directory there where they dump their stuff for testing, but most just leave the default credentials. I know Alex and Christian both have an upload script there too where you could upload files, but it would be kind of tough to install and configure it that way. You'd need a shell for that. But you said you found it there. How?"

"VPN access to the network. Your little bug was transmitting on an atypical port, so I did a port scan of the whole network until I found the right host. After that it was just simple packet sniffing to see where incoming traffic originated. By the way, is it normal for business guys to have SSH access to your servers?"

"Not surprising. Even the janitor has access to our servers probably. Anyway, I guess you have to go back in and take a closer look."

"I don't suppose you still have access?"

"No, they deactivated my remote access already, sorry. But if you do find a way, I can give you my credentials. Our admins are pretty slow, so I bet they still work. The username is mkaminski and the password is 'Ihatepasswordrules46!' all together with no spaces, all lowercase except for the first letter and an exclamation mark at the end. I should be in the sudoers list too on most servers, so you should be able to peek into the syslogs and stuff."

"How generous. Why the change of heart? You didn't seem too keen to help out earlier."

"Hey, I told you I'm innocent, and if you can get in and see that I wasn't logged in at the time the malware was installed you'll finally leave me in peace, right?"

"That's what you want? And here I was thinking this was the beginning of a beautiful friendship. Sure, if I find you're telling the truth then this'll be the last you see of this handsome mug, and I'm sure an upstanding fellow like you has got nothing to worry about."

CHAPTER 23

A jackhammer to the head would have been gentler than the throbbing migraine Antonio Rizzo was suffering. With his forehead cradled in one palm he took another sip from his coffee mug. How many cups did that make now? Five? Six? He supposed he could be glad he had a bladder like a camel. He set his mug back on the table a little too roughly, and the sound excited the little gremlins dancing around in his skull.

How many times had he watched this camera footage now? It must have been at least a hundred times. In the first video, the robot walks into Grayson's office at 11:23, passing by the Harper girl on the way, and then steps out at 11:46. In the next video it makes its way back into the office at 2:03 p.m. and at 2:14 it wanders back out. Finally, at 8:32 in the evening, the machine enters the office for the last time and strolls casually back out at 8:43. Nothing interesting there, and yet why did he keep watching these feeds?

Rizzo swiveled around in his chair hoping to ask for Lawrence's opinion only to find the young detective's ergonomic stool vacant at his desk. Rizzo's arms suddenly grew 20 kilos heavier and his shoulders slumped halfway down to his hips. He sighed and turned back to his computer.

The sergeant stabbed his fingers into his eyes and massaged them roughly. His chair groaned like an old man when he leaned back in it, holding a manila envelope with a police report he had printed out earlier in the morning. The incident had occurred Tuesday afternoon, but the reporting officer hadn't bothered to file it until Friday morning, which was just a few hours ago. Apparently the Harper girl had been telling the truth about this supposed 'hitman'. The officer had come at the beckon of the robot who had reported a shooting in an alley downtown a few blocks from the Orion Center. There wasn't much information in the report besides a description of the attacker which seemed to line up with what Rizzo had witnessed the night before. There was no mention of a note dropped by the gunman.

"Who are you?" Rizzo asked the paper in a raspy whisper.

"It's paper, not a smartphone, old man," laughed Lt. Costa, slapping Rizzo hard on the back. "It's not gonna answer you."

"Shut up," barked the older detective. "Do something useful while you're here. Pull up that chair and take a look at this, will you?"

"What, got some computer problems?" The lieutenant wore a stupid smile that Rizzo would have loved to use for target practice, but he restrained himself.

"Just shut up and look at this." Rizzo played the second and third video, fast-forwarding to the parts where the robot was on-screen. "Anything stand out to you there?"

"Not really, why?"

"I don't mean within the video itself, but compare the two of them. What's wrong with this picture?"

Costa shrugged and said, "They look the same to me."

"Yeah..." Rizzo folded his arms and rested his chin in his hand.

The younger cop stared at him, waiting for him to do something, but when he didn't, Costa rolled his eyes and stood back up. He smacked Rizzo on the back once more, disrupting his concentration, and said, "Your mind is starting to go, old man. Don't work yourself so hard."

Rizzo ignored him and tried to get back on board his train of thought. 'They look the same to me'. That had been Rizzo's observation as well. They looked exactly the same. In both cases the robot enters the room, setting its feet in exactly the same places on the floor in exactly the same way. In both videos, the robot emerges eleven minutes later and casually strolls back across the hallway. At first when he noticed it he thought it was just a robot thing. Maybe androids tend to select the same path every time. An engineer might have simply written it off as being the result of a deterministic system, one in which no randomness is involved in the process.

But somehow Rizzo hadn't been able to let it go. He continued to watch that footage over and over in the most boring carousel ride of his life, searching for some difference in the background to differentiate them. What bugged him the most wasn't the sameness of the second two videos, but that in the first video the robot had moved differently, both on its way in and out. Perhaps the difference of motion on the way in could be attributed to the machine's passing of the Harper girl, but what about its stroll back out of the office?

The detective absentmindedly lifted his mug to his lips again. When the cool rim of the container touched his mouth he slipped out of his trance and noticed the cup in his hand. Empty. Rizzo sighed.

He stood up a little too quickly and had to grab hold of his head to keep his world from spinning. The detective trudged across the room to the coffee machine and stood in front of it. The break room smelled like burnt leaves and the countertop was sticky with a week's worth of spills. He set down his cup and then hesitated. Forensics was just around the corner. Maybe he ought to drop by for a quick visit.

After a long moment of indecision, Rizzo abandoned his sad little cup and went over to the next room. He knocked on the open metal door, the tinny clank echoing like shattering glass in his ears.

"Hey guys, got a minute?" asked Rizzo.

"Oh hi Toni," replied Murphy cheerfully. He was wearing a t-shirt with the logo from some IT conference tucked into his beltless jeans. "You need something?"

"Well, yeah I guess so. Which one of you was working on the Grayson case?"

"That was me," replied Murphy.

"Great, I have a few questions if you've got a minute."

Murphy looked for a moment like he forgot how to breathe and then he swallowed, choked on it and coughed, and then it all seemed to come back to him. "I-uh, well you see I'm actually pretty busy right now. Daniels wanted me to analyze a couple of phones he picked up and I was supposed to have it done yesterday."

"Don't worry about Daniels. I'll tell him I kept you busy."

"I dunno. I don't want to disturb the other guys. We're all behind schedule right now because of that network downtime, you know?"

Rizzo sighed, "Seriously? We can go to the meeting room across the hall. Come on, Murphy, you've got more excuses than my daughter when I tell her to clean her room."

"If you had a robot around the house she wouldn't have to clean her room."

"Don't try to change the subject. What's with you today?"

Murphy glanced over to his colleagues who didn't seem to have even noticed Rizzo's presence. "Okay, let's go across the hall." He started towards the door and then stopped to bring his computer with him.

The meeting room consisted of a small round table about a meter in diameter with four of the worst chairs in the Midwest. On the wall was an old worn-out whiteboard with some indecipherable scribbles which resembled a map. In the corner of the whiteboard someone had drawn a Thanksgiving turkey in a police uniform with a thick moustache on its dangling snood and a badge that read Sgt. Rizzo. The detective frowned, but had to admit that it had been skillfully drawn.

"So, uh, what did you want to know?" asked Murphy nervously.

"Did you have a look at that computer we found at Sophie Harper's place yet?"

Murphy seemed to relax a little as he said, "Yeah, I checked it this morning. Nothing really too interesting. It belonged to Ethan Willis. You went to see him the other day, right?"

"Right. Did you find anything else?"

"There was some computer virus on it. Technically it's not a 'virus', but I won't go into the details about the differences."

"Thanks for that. And? What did it do and who put it there?"

"No idea. It seems like it was meant to transmit data, but it's not really possible to tell at this point what it may have already done. You know how we normally examine devices offline so software can't delete itself or corrupt the system?" Rizzo shook his head. "Well anyway, normally I would have waited for you before turning it on to see what the thing was actually doing, but you were busy and I got impatient, so I did it already. Looks like it was transmitting data to an IP registered to Orion Industries here downtown."

"Hm," hummed Rizzo. "Thanks. Good work, Murphy."

"Sure. Anything else you need?"

"Yeah. You examined the camera footage right?"

"Yeah," replied Murphy looking like he just sniffed a particularly sour fart.

"All of it?"

"I think so, yeah."

Rizzo pointed to the techie's tablet and said, "Pull up the footage from the camera outside Grayson's office."

Murphy grimaced like a man asked to pull something up from a clogged drain. The videos appeared on the touchscreen. "What about it?"

"You verified the authenticity of this stream?"

"Sure."

"Could you explain that?"

"Well, I looked for pattern discrepancies in the noise from the camera, but there was nothing. I adjusted the levels and contrast but didn't detect any anomalies. The shadows lined up. I did some computations to calculate the trajectories but they seemed reasonable from a physics standpoint. And then—"

"Hold it," interrupted Rizzo impatiently. "Some of those were definitely words, but I have no idea what you're talking about. English please."

Murphy raised an eyebrow and very slowly said, "Video not look fake."

"Wise-ass," grumbled the detective. "Pull up the footage from 2:03 p.m. and 8:32 p.m. Can you run those side-by-side somehow?"

"Um, I, uh…" stuttered Murphy looking flustered like a dog trying to operate the device. "Okay." He opened the two videos and played them together. They nearly lined up perfectly with the video on the left just a few seconds ahead of the other one.

"Doesn't that strike you as odd?"

"Does what?"

"Murphy, pay attention."

"I am paying attention."

The detective growled. His head was killing him and he was in no mood for nonsense. "If I have to repeat the question I'm gonna break that tablet over your hard head."

"Okay, okay. Take it easy. The videos look pretty similar. That's what you're saying, right?"

"Don't try to be cute, Murph. Those videos are exactly the same."

Murphy shrugged unconvincingly while trying hard to keep his eyes away from both the video and from the other man in the room.

"Did you compare them?" asked the detective.

"Sure."

"Did you document that?"

"Well...no."

"Why not?"

"It didn't seem necessary, I mean I already checked for anomalies in the—"

"In the noise blah blah. Right. Compare the videos."

"Toni..."

"Do it!"

Murphy let out a shaky sigh and he seemed to shrink a couple of sizes, suddenly looking small in his chair. "You're right, okay? The videos are one-to-one the same down to the pixel."

"What does that mean?"

"It means that one of them is a copy. Actually, the last one, at 8 something is the copy. If you look at the video about five minutes before the robot appears you can see the lighting flicker just the slightest bit from one frame to the next. That's where the video was inserted in place of whatever was there before."

It was as if someone had released the pressure seal on a dam and blood suddenly flooded through Rizzo's veins, instantly curing him of his migraine. The detective's arm shot across the table and caught a fist full of t-shirt, pulling Murphy out of his chair. The younger man's hands slapped clumsily on the table while he attempted to brace himself.

"Are you saying you knew this whole time?" growled Rizzo in a low voice.

"I'm sorry, I-I—"

"Talk!"

"S-someone p-paid me to look the other way."

"Who paid you?"

"I dunno, I swear! He didn't tell me his name."

"Damnit, Murphy," cursed Rizzo, pushing the man back down into his seat. "What did he look like?"

"I don't know. I only heard his voice. He called me on my personal phone. No idea how he got the number. I-I even tried to trace the call but it was from a prepaid phone."

"How much did he give you?"

"T-ten thousand."

"Christ, Murphy. You covered up forged evidence for only ten big ones? That's less than you make in a week." Rizzo tried to wipe the disappointment off his face with his palm, but it was caked on pretty hard. "Did you already get the money?"

"Yeah, but it came from some online service, not a bank account, so you can't tell who sent it."

Rizzo sighed loudly. "All right, here's what you're gonna do. You're going to go back to your desk and write up a new report. Say you screwed up and missed something and that this footage has been tampered with. I want it done within the hour. Understood?"

"Y-you're not gonna tell anyone, are you?" Murphy stared at the detective with sparkly, pleading eyes like a stupid kitten that thought it was normal wear jeans pulled up to your belly button with a t-shirt tucked into it.

"I have to think about it. Just fix that report." Murphy stared at Rizzo fearfully and the detective barked, "What are you waiting for? Get back to work!"

Murphy scurried off back to his rat's nest of wires and tech while Rizzo remained in the little meeting room. He leaned back in the chair staring unseeingly at his turkey counterpart on the whiteboard. The Harper girl had fed him exactly what he had wanted to hear. She had given him a possible motive for the robot murdering Grayson. It had been like gasoline on a fire and he had thrived on it, but as much as he loved the idea, when he flung it at the wall it just wouldn't stick.

If the android had gone back to see Grayson to kill him because of this hitman's note, why did the cameras need to be tampered with? And why did someone want it covered up? Who was behind the bribe?

Rizzo had been so ecstatic about finally having a case where he could show just how bad machines really are, and yet now here he was considering the possibility that the robot was a victim. What was going on here? And more importantly, what was going on with him? Ever since the night before he had a strange feeling he couldn't shake. He couldn't bring himself to admit it out loud, but he felt somehow, and begrudgingly, indebted to this machine which had, willingly or not, saved his backside. The detective didn't quite understand his own thoughts yet, but all he knew was that he had more questions than ever.

CHAPTER 24

Union Station was busier than a beehive on amphetamines, men and women rushing like madmen to save that extra three minutes. Every year the city seemed more crowded than the last, and places like this terminal were focal points where all the insanity and frenzy climaxed. Sometimes Seven liked to come here and sit in the Great Hall, observing the frantic bipedal animals as a reminder of the chaos of society. Today he was here for a different reason.

He made his way across the hall, only colliding with two people along the way. The detective selected one of the empty lockers along the wall and waved his credit card in front of the scanner on the front. The door popped open.

Seven stared into the dark rectangular cavern for a moment, motionless. He knew what he needed to do. It was the only rational option, and yet he hesitated. Finally, he shrugged off his coat, folded it up neatly, and placed it into the locker. He opened a small compartment on the underside of his forearm and placed the credit card inside. The android made that sideways frown he had copied from Vic and then set his hat on top of the tan pile of cloth.

Feeling strangely naked, the silver man stared into the locker longingly. He had no acceptable explanation for it, but nevertheless he found it hard to let go of these artifacts. The illogicalness of it made him feel dirty. Finally, with a tremendous effort, he forced himself to close the locker door and walk away, assuming the formal, proper gait of a cybernetic personal assistant. It felt like betrayal.

It was only half a kilometer to cross the river to reach the Orion Center, so Seven made the journey on foot. He scolded himself for having not already examined that server more closely when he had visited it before from Sophie's living room. He had been lazy and careless. Then again, if he had spent any longer investigating perhaps he would have missed his new masked buddy, and then he wouldn't have had the chance to take a peek into Willis's computer.

It was no use crying over an oil spill; what was done was done, and until they invented the time machine there was nothing that could be done to change it. For now, Seven needed to concentrate on the task at hand. He needed to find out how that software had gotten onto one of Orion's servers and who had put it there. Who was this 'BlackAlice' who had so easily infiltrated Kaminski's mind? The android's inner hacker shook its head sadly at the thought of how easily a smart guy like Kaminski had been duped by some social engineer online.

Seven entered the concrete mountain and stepped across the fine entrance hall. It was a strange thing for him to go so unnoticed. Not a single head turned his way. He was just another appliance. One of many. Not even the secretary stopped him when he walked past the desk and summoned the elevator.

The lift brought him to the R & D department where he had been just a few days before. Just three days after the murder of one of the top officials in this very building and business was already back to its same old monotony it seemed. Programmers poked at their displays and tapped on the keyboards projected on their desks. A cluster of women stood by the coffee machine chatting. Seven was invisible.

The android needed to find a computer terminal, so he stopped the first person he passed and, in a polite, gentle, tinny voice, he asked, "Hello, sir. I'm looking for the desk of Mr. Kaminski. Could you direct me to it?"

"Oh, uh. He doesn't work here anymore," said a well-groomed young man with round gold frames resting on his nose.

"That is correct. I was sent to cleanse his terminal and collect his personal affects which were left behind."

"Ah, okay, sure. He used to sit right over there. See, between that tall guy on the end and the big plant."

"Thank you," said Seven, feeling ashamed for speaking like he used to when he was new. "Have a nice day, sir."

The android sat in Kaminski's chair and booted up his computer. When prompted, he entered the programmer's username and password, which the machine happily accepted and welcomed him to the system. Seven pulled up a console and connected to the server where he had found the malware. After a brief scan he located the program saved with a generic name in a generic path. According to the timestamps, the program was placed there on Monday, the day before the murder, and well after Kaminski was fired. About thirty people had logged in that day, including mkaminski. Either the programmer had lied to him, or perhaps the fool had shared his password with BlackAlice as well as his code.

The detective shut down the computer and asked the man in the next cube for directions to IT operations. The administrators were sitting one floor below, so Seven climbed down to visit them. The room was smaller than the one above, and spare cables and equipment took up more space than the people did. Seven identified the man he judged to be the most likely to be forthcoming, eating a peanut butter and jelly sandwich, giggling at something on his screen.

"Hello, sir," greeted Seven. The man started and quickly attempted to close some video playing. When he noticed it was just a robot he relaxed. "I'm sorry to disturb you while you eat, but I hoped to inquire as to the state of Mr. Kaminski's access."

"Really? They've never sent down a robot to ask about that before," said the man suspiciously.

"Mr. Kaminski was terminated under atypical circumstances, and it was Mr. Grayson's last instruction to me to ensure that he would not be able to obtain access to the network of Orion Industries. Mr. Grayson believed that Mr. Kaminski may try to retaliate in some way."

"Oh, okay," said the admin, content with Seven's fabricated explanation. "Well, Max's user hasn't been deleted yet on all our servers, but we deactivated his email and his intranet access, and we disabled his VPN access last week."

Seven cocked his head instinctively, considered straightening it out of habit, and then reconsidered and left it crooked. "When last week?"

"Last Thursday I think. Let me check....Yeah, Thursday afternoon. So he shouldn't be able to get into our network anymore from outside, and definitely nobody is going to let him back in the building. But still, I'll raise the priority on the ticket to delete his user. Fine?"

"Yes, thank you. Have a nice day." Seven started to walk away, but then stopped again one step into his exit. He spun around and asked, "Supposing Mr. Kaminski did somehow log into one of those servers this week, how might that have occurred?"

The admin looked irritated. "What do you mean?"

"You're certain that the VPN access was revoked last week?"

"I did it myself."

"And there are no unprotected servers which can be accessed from outside the network?"

"Of course not. Look, like I said, the only way he could do anything is if he was here in the building or if someone shared their access with him, and I really doubt either of those things would happen. Nobody liked Kaminski, so they wouldn't help him, and we have two-factor authentication, so just knowing someone's VPN password wouldn't be enough. Tell whoever it was that sent you to relax."

"Mr. Grayson sent me, and I doubt he's going to get any more relaxed than he is now." Seven realized he may have slipped away from the character he was attempting to play while in the background wondering which was him and which was the character. He quickly added, "Thank you for your time, sir. Have a nice day."

Seven returned to the developers one floor higher. The three women he had observed earlier were still gabbing by the coffee machine. Everyone sitting within a five-meter radius of them wore massive noise-cancelling headphones. Seven approached the women.

"Good afternoon, ladies," Seven greeted with a slight bow. "May I borrow a moment of your time please?"

The women looked at one another confused and the blonde in the middle said, "Uh, sure."

"I've been sent by HR to conduct a brief survey concerning work-life balance within the company. Would you be willing to participate? Your answers would be completely anonymous."

The three exchanged another glance and they all shrugged. The blonde said, "Sure, I guess so."

"Perfect. Before we begin, do you all work here in the R&D department?"

"Yes," replied the woman on the right who looked about ten years older than the other two.

"In which roles?"

"I'm the product owner of the nanotech team," replied the blonde. "Christina is QA, and Laura is a developer in the cybernetics team."

"Excellent," replied Seven. "This survey has been initiated in response to the recent termination of Mr. Kaminski last week. Did you know him?"

"Yes we all knew him," answered the blonde.

"Did he have many friends here at Orion?"

The blonde deferred to the other two, and it was the older woman, Laura, who answered, "Not really. He wasn't very well-liked here, but we all had a sort of respect for him. He sometimes said things that we were all thinking, you know?"

"I see, and what was his relationship with Mr. Grayson?"

"Nothing good. They hated each other. Honestly I'm surprised Max didn't get fired sooner with the way he talked to Grayson."

"Were there many such conflicts here in the workplace?"

Laura thought for a moment and then said, "With Grayson there were always conflicts. He was a hard guy to get along with, or so I've heard at least, I never had to deal with him directly. Besides that though not really. Like in any workplace there are things to complain about, but it's okay overall."

Seven looked to the other two who nodded but added nothing. "How do you feel is the general mood here in the workplace?"

The blonde answered, "It's pretty good from my perspective. We get to build cool, new, state-of-the-art tech every day, and every day is a new challenge."

The QA girl, Christina, rolled her eyes and said, "What we're building was state-of-the-art ten years ago." Laura nodded silently.

Seven paused briefly to allow more opportunity for the women to speak before posing his next question. "What would you say the typical working hours are in this department?"

"It depends a little," said Laura. "I usually come in at 8 and leave at about 4:30, I think Christina is here from about 10 till

6." She nodded towards the blonde and said, "Madison is usually here when I get here and she stays pretty late, till like 6:30. Right?"

"Do you ever stay later than that?"

"Later than 6:30?" asked Madison. "No, not usually, and I'm usually one of the last to leave."

"Have you ever heard of Ethan Willis?" asked Seven. He watched the three carefully for any signs of recognition. They all shook their heads. "He's a medical researcher who recently published a paper claiming that working more than 50 hours per week increases your risk of stroke by 33 percent, and he indicates a correlation with depression, insomnia, and diabetes."

"Oh," said Madison.

"Thank you very much for your time, ladies. Have a nice day." Seven walked away, leaving the three woman looking slightly confused. As he reached the elevator he could hear them giggling.

Seven rode the elevator up three floors to Business Analytics, where Sophie Harper worked. Just to be on the safe side, he asked if she was there, and was told that she had taken the week off. Seven found two men in an office who were having a friendly conversation about some TV series. He tapped lightly on the glass door and then entered.

"Hello gentlemen, may I interrupt shortly?" Neither answered, so he continued. "After the recent tragedy which occurred on Tuesday night, Human Resources saw it fit to offer a grief counseling program. I would like to shortly introduce the program to you and to ask a few questions so that we can effectively calibrate the sessions."

The two men grimaced, clearly about as enthusiastic to listen to him as they were to resume the work they were being paid to do. Seven asked, "Did either of you work closely with Mr. Grayson?"

"I don't know if you could say closely," said the man with a thick beard like a lumberjack, the curly brown hair making a soft scratching sound as it brushed across his white shirt, "but yeah he was our boss's boss."

"How do you feel about the recent tragedy?"

The bearded man shrugged and said, "It was a surprise. I never knew someone who got murdered before."

"What about Ms. Harper. Did you know her?"

"Yeah she works here on this floor, why?"

"She's been written ill for the whole week because of grief. Was she close to Mr. Grayson in your opinion?"

"Naw," laughed the other man, a pale, skinny fellow with a sausage-shaped mole on his cheek. "She was terrified of him. Every time she had to talk to him she came back down here looking like she was having an asthma attack."

"I see. Is it typical to work nights in this department?"

"No, not really. Sophie did every once in a while because she freaks out when something isn't finished, but that's still pretty rare. Jason Monroe sometimes stays late too, but usually not later than 7 or 8."

"How would you characterize the general atmosphere in the department since the tragedy?"

"Sort of quiet I guess. Nobody really talks about it much. I mean, they do, but in a pretty hushed tone, you know?"

"Have you ever heard of Ethan Willis?" asked Seven, again watching for any kind of reaction. Both men shook their heads.

"He says that a man cannot selectively numb his grief any more than he can turn out the lights and still expect to see. Thank you for your time gentlemen. You'll be hearing from someone upstairs again next week when we present the program to the company. Have a nice day."

Seven walked away, glad the last of his acting was behind him. Pretending to be a mindless automaton felt like a betrayal of himself and even worse, like a betrayal of Vic. Vic had worked so hard to raise Seven to be what he was now, and to go back to how he once was, even if it was just an act, felt wrong.

He floated up a few more floors until he reached the level containing the office of the late Miles Grayson. All that was left to do now was to search the office. He expected that it had already been scoured clean by the cops, but he had to be sure. Seven would leave no stone unturned.

CHAPTER 25

Feeling slightly drunk in that way he always did when a bad headache finally let up, Rizzo hopped out of the police cruiser and told it to come back for him in two hours. The vehicle sealed itself and drove away to wherever it was cars went to socialize. With his hands in his pockets and his neck retreated as far down into his coat as possible, Rizzo approached the sparkling glass entrance of the Orion Center.

He wasn't really sure what he was looking for, but it had seemed to him to be the only reasonable place to look. Someone had played around with the cameras, and until now nobody had known it, so it was an avenue still unexplored. In addition to that, Murphy had mentioned some sort of computer bug talking to someone in this building. The detective wondered if that may have been the original reason for the robot coming here.

Rizzo pulled open the glass door, feeling a little flustered for having difficulties lifting it. Stupid obnoxiously heavy door. He took one step onto the smooth marble floor when a thick hand like a cinder block pushed his chest firmly.

"What's your business?" came a deep voice that sounded like words with more than one syllable came with difficulty. The bouncer was a tall orange-haired thug with shoulders like an elephant. He was wearing a black suit. An ink snake held the man's thick neck in its deadly coils.

The detective unzipped his coat and reached inside for his badge. The bouncer's eyes widened and his face contorted into a furious expression as he placed his hand on the gun hanging from his belt.

"Whoa whoa, take it easy, guy," said Rizzo putting both hands open in front of him. "I'm a cop. I wanted to show you my badge. I'm going to reach inside my coat and take it out, okay?" Rizzo did as he said, slowly with no sudden moves. He pulled out his shiny golden shield.

The bouncer let his hand fall back to his side after studying the badge briefly. His nostrils flared like they had been infiltrated by some potent stink. Rizzo waited for a moment for an acknowledgement, but received none. The detective started walking again and this time the big guy let him pass.

Shaking his head, the detective headed deeper into the heart of the lobby. As he passed the front desk a cheerful female voice called out to him.

"Sir? I need to you to sign in first."

Rizzo sighed and approached the receptionist.

"May I ask what your business is here at the Orion Center today?" asked the robot with a smile.

Rizzo flashed her his badge and said, "I'm Sergeant Antonio Rizzo from the Chicago PD. I'm here to follow up on the investigation of the murder of Miles Grayson."

"Okay, great. Do you have an appointment?"

"What do you mean?"

"Do you have an appointment with Mr. Grayson?"

"You're not serious," said Rizzo in disbelief.

"Of course I am, silly. Mr. Grayson is a very busy man." The machine ended with a dopy smile and cocked its head.

Rizzo furrowed his brow and in a tone like he was talking to a moron, he explained, "Miles Grayson has been dead since Tuesday."

The gynoid look confused for a moment and then repeated, "Mr. Grayson is a very busy man."

The detective shook his head and gave up trying to talk to it. He started to walk towards the elevator. The robot called out, "Sir, if you don't stop I'm afraid I'll have to call security."

Rizzo looked back over his shoulder at the meathead who had stopped him on his way in. He decided he wasn't in the mood for a discussion with a brick wall, so he turned back and said, "I do have an appointment."

"No you don't Mr. Rizzo. I've checked Mr. Grayson's schedule and he has no appointments with you today."

"I want to speak to a person," demanded Rizzo.

"I can call someone to reception for you if you like. Who would you like to talk to?"

"I don't know. Who normally does your maintenance? Installing updates and all that."

"Someone from IT Operations usually does that. I'm not allowed to reveal any names. Would you like me to call someone from IT Operations?"

"Yes. Do that." Rizzo decided he was okay with that outcome. He needed to talk to someone from IT anyway about the cameras.

"Okay great. I'm calling someone right now. Please have a seat over there and someone will come to see you." The robot gestured to a row of comfy looking armchairs in the center of the lobby.

Rizzo spent the next twenty minutes playing some inane game on his phone that his daughter had gotten him addicted to. He smiled slightly, feeling triumphant for beating his high score, when a portly young man in a t-shirt and jeans approached him. Rizzo looked up at him, but the man just stared at down at his own sneakers. The husky man found them far more fascinating than Rizzo did.

"Are you the guy from IT?" asked the detective.

"Yes," he replied, his eyes still on the floor. "You're a cop?"

"That's right," said Rizzo, standing up. He jerked a thumb to his right toward the front desk. "What's the deal with the receptionist? It thinks Grayson is still alive."

"Oh, she's a little bit messed up right now," explained the young man, seeming slightly more relaxed now that the conversation had landed on a topic within his comfort zone. He was so relaxed, in fact, that he even chanced a quick glance at the detective's worn-out black loafers. "She's been a little funky all week. Whoever screwed with her memory on Tuesday night did a crappy job and now she's totally confused. She still thinks it's Monday for some reason, and she doesn't seem to be able to commit anything to long-term memory anymore. We're waiting for someone from the manufacturer to come out and run a diagnostic."

"Hmm, I see. And do you have any ideas who could have wiped her memory like that? Who has access?"

"Well..." The techie seemed hesitant to continue, so he just stopped there hoping he had said enough.

"Well?"

The young man looked Rizzo in the face for an instant and, with an expression almost akin to panic his eyes darted back down to the marble floor. "I normally install all her updates, but I installed a custom program for it to make it easier and so that others can do it if I'm sick or on vacation. We use the same program sometimes to clear her memories on purpose too."

"Why would you do that?"

"Well sometimes we have clients who want to be discrete, and sometimes we get clients who just don't want to be recorded by a robot and who don't trust the enforcement of

U.S. privacy regulations. Mostly Europeans. So yeah, sometimes we clear her memories for a couple hours after that."

"And the machine always gets kooky like that after a wipe?"

"Well no, but like I said it's also the same app I use for installing updates and reconfiguring her, so maybe someone just mashed some buttons without knowing what they were doing and borked her system, you know? I guess in hindsight I ought to have restricted the admin parts..."

"Who has access to this app?"

"Everyone in operations and most people who deal with external clients. That's about a hundred people I guess."

Rizzo sighed and said, "All right. Can you bring me upstairs?"

The detective stood by the desk of a man with sandy blonde hair and a pink strawberry jam stain on his white shirt that he didn't seem conscious of. The man was tapping at the keys projected onto his table while controlling the focus of the windows on the holographic display with rapid motions from his eyes.

"See, it's like I told you," he said defensively. "There's nothing."

"According to my forensics guy—," who at this point he wasn't sure was reliable, "—there's some computer bug which is talking to something here on one of your servers."

"I'm completely sure there's nothing," the admin insisted.

"If you check it I'll let you tell that to my guy personally. How's that sound?" The man frowned. "Otherwise I'll have to come back with a warrant and then you have to give our forensics team access and they definitely don't leave the place cleaner than it was when they got there once they start snooping around. Up to you." Rizzo was pretty sure forensics would be taking a gander of their own regardless, but he hoped these guys might be a little quicker about it.

The admin sighed and said, "Fine, I'll check." He started doing something and then stopped and looked at Rizzo with an annoyed expression. "You should come back later. It'll take a while."

"Okay, could someone bring me to the camera room?"

"The what?"

"The room with all the monitors showing the camera feeds."

The admin chuckled and said, "You watch too much TV, dude. We don't have a room like that."

"But then where do the camera feeds go?"

"They go to one of our servers here in the building. You can access it from anywhere if you have the right privileges."

"Who has access?"

"Well, there's an application that you can install on your computer which connects to the server for viewing, backing up, and deleting footage. Tom Curtis, the security officer, sits down the hall; he's the superuser. And the guards downstairs and the receptionist have read access. So do the big bosses like Grayson and Morris. That's about it though." His head ping-ponged side-to-side between two invisible paddles and he added, "Well, technically the admins and devs also have direct access to the server."

"That means this Tom Curtis, you guys here, and the developers would all be theoretically able to modify the footage?"

"Well, y-yeah I guess so. But why would anyone do that?"

"That's what I'm trying to find out. Are there any sort of access logs for this server?"

"Sure."

"Could you check it?"

A loud, harsh sigh slashed through the quiet ambiance of the room "Which do you want me to do, check the logs or hunt for this non-existent virus?"

"I want you to do both. You said the other thing will take a while, so do this first and then I'll get out of your hair. That fine with you?"

The admin pouted angrily and Rizzo thought he might throw a tantrum. Instead he typed a few things into the console and about two minutes later his eyes opened wide like he had seen a ghost.

"Something wrong?"

"Uh, n-no, nothing wrong. It's just...hmm..." He started flipping through open programs with short motions from his eyes and head, occasionally typing something.

"Is some kind of explanation coming?" asked Rizzo patiently.

The admin frowned. "On Tuesday night there was a login by someone who used to work here. But actually it shouldn't be possible. I revoked his VPN access last week, so he shouldn't be able to login from outside. Man, the one time HR sends someone down to check it..."

"Who was this guy who logged in?" Rizzo pulled his little notebook out of his coat pocket and flipped it open.

"His name is Max Kaminski. He was fired last week and got into a pretty big fight with...oh!" The admin's eyes blew up wide.

"With who?"

"With Grayson!"

CHAPTER 26

Grayson's computer was password protected. After five bad guesses it locked itself saying to try again in an hour or contact an administrator. Seven turned his attention to the other objects in the room. There wasn't much to see.

Seven spent a few minutes sifting through the short stack of tablets beside the computer. Just reports about various clients or potential acquisitions, most of which were significantly more verbose than necessary. There were no further objects visible in the room. Beneath the table, however, was a thin drawer which was somehow not visible through the glass tabletop. Probably a projection.

Seven pulled open the drawer. It was filled with random odds and ends, like how a child stuffs everything under the bed when it cleans its room. Seven picked up a full bottle of toothpaste to better sort through the drawer.

The office door opened. Antonio Rizzo walked in, clearly expecting the room to be empty. When he saw a robot sitting at Grayson's desk holding onto a bottle of toothpaste he froze in his tracks. Seven sat perfectly motionless under Rizzo's gorgon glare. The two remained perfectly still for an eternity. Empires have risen, conquered, and fallen in a shorter time span.

Finally, Rizzo broke the silence. "It's you." His hand fumbled at the door handle behind him, eventually getting a grasp and then pulling it closed. The officer drew his sidearm and pointed it loosely at the android.

"Greetings, sir," said Seven cheerfully. "Can I help you?"

"Drop the act, I know it's you."

"While it's true that I am me, I do not know to which act you refer. Could you be more specific?"

"Don't be coy. I've seen you twice now. Coat or not, I recognize you."

"All of us from the X series look quite similar. Is it not possible you're mistaken? Also I'm afraid I'll have to ask you to lower your weapon. The Orion Center is a gun-free setting."

"Come on, quit messing around. Look, I just want to talk. That's all."

"What would you like to talk about? I've been programmed with over 14 million conversation topics in 12 languages." There was a panic button under the table. Seven briefly considered pressing it to call security, but he hesitated, deciding that would likely just lead to things getting messy.

"Vic Sinclair is your owner, right?" asked Rizzo looking slightly uncertain. He lowered his weapon but didn't sheath it.

Seven showed no sign that he heard the question.

"You know," continued the sergeant, "I had been thinking that name sounded really familiar so I did a little digging around and then it hit me. I met a man named Victor Sinclair about 15 years ago. He was a cop back then, working a case for the 12th district which crossed over with one of my cases." He paused to allow a response but none came. The robot could have been a silver statue.

"Back then I was in my prime. The mayor hated me, and every mobster in town knew my name. But Sinclair, now there was a guy with five aces in his hand. Sinclair didn't need any blood spatter analyst or computer forensic specialists; they couldn't tell him anything he hadn't figured out first. This guy was sharper than a barber's razor blade. He was an entire police force on two feet.

"I had been working this case on and off for three months. Some low level drug dealer turned up dead in some grimy back alley. It wasn't anything out of the ordinary, so I had mostly written it off as an upset customer or rival gang thing. The only reason I kept coming back to it was the murder weapon.

"You ever heard of a kunai? It's a small Japanese blade, originally a tool used by farmers, but later used by ninjas. You probably already looked that up online while I was talking, right? Anyway, we found one sticking out of the guy's back. Seemed pretty strange to me, but then again, addicts are a strange kind of people.

"Three months later this hotshot, Sinclair, barges into the station wanting to talk to me about this dealer. He said he was investigating a missing person who had my dead dealer on speed dial. So I show him the file and he takes one look at it and says, 'this was no disgruntled customer, this was an assassination'. Turned out he was right.

"Two weeks later we had the culprit. It turns out my dealer wasn't just some ordinary dope peddler. He and Sinclair's missing person were into some kind of jewel heist racket together with the murderer. Our perp was supposed to pawn the gems and split the win with his partners, but instead he hired an assassin to take his buddies out so he could take the whole pot.

"After just two weeks we solved his case, mine, and a jewel theft nobody even knew had occurred. Three months I kept coming back to that case and saw nothing but a dead drug dealer with a funny knife in his back. I had already made up my mind about the punk and was blind to anything else. It never occurred to me that there could be anything more to it. After that I made a promise to myself never to let myself become blinded by preconceptions again. I almost broke that promise this week."

Seven assumed this was some kind of ploy to get him to reveal himself. Maybe this old man with the well-endowed olfactory organ was telling the truth, or maybe it was all hokum. Either way it was definitely an attempt to elicit some kind of emotional response from him. Seven was unmoved. However, he was uncertain whether he would gain anything from continuing this charade.

The sergeant seemed to be implying that he was willing to consider Seven's innocence. The android classified the possibilities into just two groups: A, Rizzo is sincere; B, he's employing deception. The android's options were also two: 1, cooperate; 2, keep playing dumb. That left him with the following possible outcomes: 1A could lead to a swift resolution of the case; 1B would likely lead to Seven being arrested; 2A the two continue investigating on their own; 2B Seven probably still ends up arrested. Simplified: 1A positive, 1B negative, 2A neutral, 2B negative.

"Where is Vic now?" asked Rizzo gently.

"He's dead," stated Seven coldly in his normal voice. That was the first time he had ever said it out loud.

Rizzo put his gun away and said, "I'm sorry to hear that."

"Why?" asked Seven just to be difficult.

"I, uh, he was a good detective. One of the few good ones in the city. How long?"

"Eight months."

"You've been on your own for eight months? How? Who paid the bills? Why weren't his accounts frozen?"

"It's touching that you drove all the way here just to discuss my finances."

"You're right, you're right. That's not important right now."

"You solve the case yet?" asked Seven, mostly in mockery.

"I'm not sure. I've got a good lead now. You?"

"Not quite. I take it this means you've realized I was framed?"

"I'm starting to think you were." The detective ran his fingers through his hair and looked away. "I can't believe I'm saying this, but what if we worked together on this? There are definitely things you know that I don't, and maybe I know a thing or two you haven't figured out."

Seven couldn't be sure this wasn't some kind of trick, but again, he decided he had less to lose by cooperating than by being rebellious. "All right. You first."

"Well like I said, I don't know much. The camera footage was faked. That much you know, I guess. What you probably don't know was that forensics also knew about it and kept quiet because someone paid them off."

"Any idea who?" asked Seven looking interested.

"No. A man called from a prepaid phone. The money was transferred through some anonymous online service. Sounded professional."

"Okay," said the android looking bored again.

"It sounds like the camera footage was modified by an ex-developer from here named Max Kaminski. Did you know that?"

"No, but I'm not surprised. Kaminski's user seems to have gotten around."

"Care to explain what you mean by that?"

Seven didn't really care to. Explaining things verbally was a slow, tedious task that often led to misunderstandings. He supposed he ought to, however. "I have to start from the beginning or else you'll be lost.

"My case began with Ethan Willis bringing me his computer which had a sizeable amount of cryptocurrency stolen from it. I detected a piece of malware transmitting to an IP belonging to Orion.

"Fast forward a while to this morning when I discovered that Kaminski created this malware and gave it to someone called BlackAlice via IRC—"

"What's IRC?

"Internet relay chat. It's not important. So Kaminski gives his code to this person who he has clearly developed a romantic interest in. Now I found that his user logged into the server where this malware was transmitting to, but after his access from outside was revoked."

"So he's our guy?"

"Could be. Or if could be he's an idiot and he gave his password to this BlackAlice character. What's odd in either case is that whoever it was that logged in was either here or had VPN access."

"So you don't think it was this Kaminski guy then?"

"I'm not sure," replied Seven. "It could be, but he didn't really seem the type to me. Plus either way all we have is circumstantial evidence. We have access logs which imply that he may have manipulated the cameras, but that doesn't prove he killed someone. And I still have no idea what this malware has to do with the whole thing. Plus he has an alibi. It's pretty weak though."

"Hmm," hummed Rizzo, stroking his moustache while casually roaming the barren office. "What about this masked shooter? You've had three encounters with this guy now, right? How does he fit into all this?"

"Another mystery."

"You don't know anything about him?"

"All I know was that the day I first met Grayson, I ran into this guy and he dropped a note with my name on it signed with Grayson's initials. Then when I went to see Willis the day after my arrest he told me he was mugged by a guy fitting the description the night before. When I ran into this masked man in West Engelwood he dropped a bag containing Willis's computer. About an hour before that apparently Willis was in that same bar meeting with Elizabeth Grayson."

Rizzo scribbled frantically in his little book. When he finally finished he said, "After that bar fight the masked man got into a cab outside the building. I traced it to South State Street and West Cermak Road, just outside of Chinatown."

That caught the android's interest. "That's about a block away from the Coliseum."

"You're thinking he might work for Caesar?"

"Elizabeth Grayson mentioned that her husband made a habit of gambling."

Looking thoughtful, Rizzo asked, "Did you maybe consider that you misunderstood that note he dropped—this hitman I mean—when you first met him? What if those initials weren't a signature, but the next item on the list?"

"You think Grayson may have been a target too?"

"It makes sense. Think about it. A hitman shows up with a list with Grayson's initials on it, and that same night he turns up dead. Caesar is exactly the kind of guy who would use a hitman, and that bribe to ignore the faked camera footage has his name all over it."

"But why was my name on the list?"

"Hmm. I don't know."

Seven stood up from the desk. "I guess I'll just have to ask him then."

"You want to walk into the Coliseum and ask Caesar if he hired someone to kill you? Self-preservation must not be in your programming."

"I'll be fine."

"I can't come with you," warned the cop.

"It's better that way. You can do me a favor though."

"Okay, what do you need?"

"Go down to the morgue where they put Grayson's body and get his belongings. Everything he had on him at the time of death."

Rizzo hesitated for a moment and then nodded slowly. "Okay, but why?"

"There's something Vic used say. Never verbalize your ideas before you have the facts. He said ideas are like a sculptor's clay, all raw and wet, still malleable. As soon as you put your idea into words and say it out loud you've turned your clay into a hard, solid sculpture, and it's not easy to add more clay on top if it or to chisel pieces away once it's hardened. Plus, once you've got your nice sculpture in front of you you're not going to want to pay any attention to the rest of those raw hunks of clay in the room anymore."

"Fine, you can have your secrets then if you don't want to share. How do I know where to meet you?"

"I'll call you when I'm ready."

Rizzo started to pull his phone from his pocket to check his number which he could never remember.

"Don't bother. I got your number while I was in the station's network. Just get that stuff for me and wait for my call."

CHAPTER 27

The Coliseum was an enormous structure that looked like what you'd get if you mated a castle with a hanger and then fed the offspring steroids. At each corner of the building stood a tall cylindrical tower made of giant stone bricks and crowned with battlements. In the center of the building, the grand entrance had an arched doorway with a small watchtower to each side of it. The doorway had a wrought iron portcullis that may have just been for show, but the spikes were nevertheless razor sharp. The roof of the building was a tall, rounded green dome that looked like it belonged on an air base. The ceiling could be retracted on nice sunny days. The ceiling had been closed for a long time.

Seven approached the main entrance together with a mass of people all lined up to watch tonight's fight. Seven hoped he could slip by unnoticed, although that was unlikely since he had dressed himself in his hat and coat once again.

"Uh uh uh," said the ticket collector, pushing Seven roughly. "No entry without a ticket."

"I don't have a ticket," stated Seven.

"Then no entry! Now skedaddle." He made a shooing motion with his hands.

"Where can I get a ticket?"

"Ticket desk's over there. Now get outta the line so we can keep this thing moving."

Seven walked to a window in one of the watchtowers beside the entrance. The box office was manned by a heavyset thug with a once white, now yellowed t-shirt. He was talking to a skinny man in a brown tweed suit with a matching beret cap and a white t-shirt beneath the coat. Skinny was an understatement; the man could have been a skeleton wearing a skin-colored gimp suit. Both men stood outside the box office, leaning casually against the window. They didn't give the appearance of being open for business, but Seven decided to try anyway.

"Evening boys," greeted the robot. "Where can a guy get tickets to this spectacle?"

"Robots ain't allowed inside," said the skinny man through the corner of his mouth. The other corner was busy sucking on a cigarette.

"Why not?" asked Seven.

"Boss don't want anyone recording the match. Them's just the rules."

"Is there any way you could make an exception? I'd really like to get inside."

The thin man's head retreated slightly like he took a soft slap to the face, and he made a face to match it. "Now why would I go and do that?"

"Say I paid you a little extra on the side?" suggested Seven slyly.

The skinny man looked at his big companion for a minute and then said, "You trying to bribe me, punk? Whaddaya think this is, the Chicago PD? Get outta here." He jerked his thumb back over his shoulder towards the street.

"Look, I don't care about the fight. I just want to talk to Caesar."

The talking skeleton turned to his pal and said, "He wants to talk to Caesar."

"Your friend there hard of hearing? I just said that."

"A wise guy, eh?" He took a step towards Seven and pulled the cigarette out of his mouth and slowly mashed it into Seven's chest. Hot ashes fluttered down to the pavement leaving a black circle on the android's breast. "Look at that, a walking ashtray. You ever seen a walking ashtray before, Rusty?"

"Nope," said Rusty with a dopey grin, ripples spreading across his big belly as he chuckled silently.

"Just call your boss and tell him the guy who busted his cousin out of the slammer on Wednesday night wants to talk to him."

"Can you believe this guy?" said the skinny man jerking his boney thumb in Seven's direction. He looked uncertain, however, and he seemed to decide better than to take any risks, so he took out his phone and dialed. "Yeah, Bones here. Yeah, I-yeah. Anyway-yeah, anyway, there's a robot down here says he's the guy busted Sheldon out of the clink earlier this week. Yeah. He wants to talk to the boss. Yeah, hmm…yeah, all right." He put his phone back into his pocket and glared at Seven.

"And?"

"Someone's coming down to meet you," he said begrudgingly. "What's some rust bucket wanna see Caesar for anyways?"

"That's between me and the big man. Stick to your pay grade, pal."

The stick man's face reddened and he stood up straight and alert. He rolled up the sleeve of his right arm. Maybe he thought showing more bone would be intimidating.

"Go on, try it," urged Seven calmly, his face a blank slate.

Bones stood there frozen with his left arm holding his right sleeve, just staring at this cheeky robot. He couldn't seem to decide whether it would be worse to lose a fight or to lose face. He didn't have to decide.

"This is the man you called about?" asked a robot who had just emerged from the watchtower. He had a notably tall, cylindrical head with a little antenna on top. He was a particularly old model, but he moved like his parts had been modernized.

"Yeah," spat Bones.

"Come," the robot instructed. Seven followed obediently.

The two androids entered through a small metal door leading into the nearest tower. From the outside one may have expected something akin to a dungeon, but inside it looked more like a casino. Thin red carpet with black and yellow rectangles scattered randomly kept the floor warm. The walls were cherry wood with occasional lamps protruding with green, cylindrical glass shades.

Seven followed his guide across the round room to an elevator with a shiny stainless steel door. The other android pressed the button for the last floor.

"Did they hassle you much?" asked the guy with the cylindrical head. He spoke with a very smooth, precise voice.

"Nothing I'm not used to," answered Seven.

"Cretins."

"I'm Seven. You got a name?" asked Seven, intrigued by his counterpart's frankness.

Can-head stared at the detective for a few milliseconds and then said, "Ajax" in a tone that made it seem like introductions were beneath him.

"You been working here long?

"For 17 years, 253 days, 9 hours, and 22 seconds."

"Huh, that's about 12 seconds longer than I was about to guess. Say, have you maybe seen a guy around here who wears a black balaclava and carries a 9 millimeter around?"

"It is not my place to discuss family matters with outsiders."

"So he's family then?"

Ajax's head turned to face the person he was speaking to for the first time. "I did not say that. I will not speak of matters that may or may not concern the family."

"You haven't left yourself much left to speak about then. You taking a vow of silence?"

"You are very difficult. Do not waste my cycles playing with the limitations of verbal language. If you have inquiries, you will need to take them up with Caesar. We are arriving presently."

The particularly slow-moving elevator dinged and came to a halt. The doors opened to a room that was decorated similarly to the one downstairs, but which contained a number of large chairs all facing a big window which slanted outwards.

A short, wide-shouldered man with a belly like a beach ball lounged in a gaudy, burgundy armchair that continued to rise a good 50 centimeters past the top of his head. He wasn't a young man, probably a few years Rizzo's senior. His skin looked weather-worn and was speckled with large, brown liver spots. The top of his head looked like a grey peach.

Julius "Caesar" Morelli wore a pale Easter-yellow shirt with the sleeves rolled up to his elbows to show the thick grey forest growing on his arms. A lavender necktie hung loosely around his neck, the noose pulled wide and the top few buttons of his shirt opened to air out. His pants were held up by bright red suspenders. The man looked rather dandy for a mobster. A fat stub of a Cuban perched itself in the corner of his mouth.

"Caesar, I presume?" greeted Seven. "You're a lot shorter than the statues."

A hush came over the room. The mob boss stared at the robot for a long while. Finally, he burst into laughter, his skin crinkling at the outer corners of his eyes from a long habit of

Scott Finlay

laughing. The cigar bobbed in his mouth, but stayed put. Whoever had glued it there had done a good job.

"Hawhaw!" laughed Caesar. "A funny guy! I like funny guys."

Caesar waved a hand, beckoning the android to come closer. "Come 'ere. Look at you. Somebody put a little hat and coat on you. Adorable!" He craned his neck around the side of his armchair and shouted, "Hey Ajax, how'd you like a hat to cover up that thingy on top of your head?"

Ajax said nothing. Caesar sat straight again and, softly to himself, said, "I'm gonna get him a hat."

The mobster raised his voice again to address Seven. He raised it about three notches higher than necessary. "You did my boy Sheldon a solid this week. Caesar is a man who repays good deeds. What can I do for you?"

"I was hoping to—"

"What's your name, robot?"

"Seven Sinclair."

"Sinclair, eh? I knew a Sinclair once," said Caesar, moving his hands in front of him like he was speaking some kind of sign language. "Bigger pain in the ass than hemorrhoids. He got me into some deep doo-doo about ten years back. I broke his kneecaps. You know the guy I'm talking about?"

Seven did. Vic had never been quite as surefooted again after that, or so his sister had told him. Vic didn't like to talk about that. "Nope. I saw the name on a billboard and thought it had a nice ring to it."

"All right. What was it you said you wanted to talk to me about?"

"I was just getting to—"

Caesar suddenly jumped out of his chair and threw a fist into an invisible enemy, laughing and shouting, "Oh yeah! Did you see the hook on that guy? Holy hell that kid's got shoulders on him."

Seven glanced down at the raised platform in the center of the room beneath. Dozens of spotlights focused on a blue square surrounded by a roped fence. It was a pen to contain two man-shaped animals that were clearly meant to be kept in separate cages.

"Did you know, this is actually the fourth Coliseum in Chicago?" asked Caesar without turning away from the glass. "I modeled the outside of mine after the third, but it was the second Coliseum that really had the heart. That thing was twice the size of Madison Square Garden, and built at a time when they actually had humans doing all the heavy lifting. Can you believe that? It was one of the greatest buildings of the 19th century. That thing had heart."

"And it only took 20 minutes to burn it to the ground just a year and a half after it opened," said Seven, hoping to immobilize the man's mouth long enough to finally state his business.

Caesar frowned but continued to stare glumly down at the arena below. A wise man probably would have stopped there. Seven continued. "Just goes to show that no matter how massive or impressive a thing—or an empire—is, it's always easier to destroy it than it was to raise it up. Just look at your namesake."

Caesar turned to face him again. "You got guts, kid."

"So I've been told. I was hoping to ask you about someone who may have come to see you last night."

"I'm listening."

"I had a minor disagreement with a man wearing a black balaclava Thursday night and he drove off before we could finish. He did most of his talking with a 9 millimeter. Does that sound like anyone you might know?"

The skin on Caesar's face tightened giving him the appearance of a man eating a grapefruit and trying not to flinch. "Don't sound like anyone I know. Ajax, you know a guy like that?"

"No, sir," answered the android still standing by the elevator.

"He drove over here after we parted ways" continued Seven. "I'd really like to find him and finish our conversation."

"Nobody came to visit me last night. There was a pretty good match though. Maybe he was a customer."

"Maybe," agreed Seven weakly. "I'll move on to the main reason I wanted to talk to you then. I was hired by a woman named Elizabeth Grayson to dig up the dirt on her husband, Miles Grayson, to use in her upcoming divorce battle. Funny thing is, the husband turned up dead Tuesday night. Now, as to who killed him and why, that's a police matter, it's none of my business. But my client wants to make sure she's not about to inherit any unwanted debts along with her new fortune. I understand Miles Grayson was something of a gambler."

"Never heard of him."

Seven doubted that. "That means I can go back to my client and tell her she's got nothing to worry about from you and your crew?"

"You can tell the lady whatever you like. I've got no business with anyone by the name of Grayson."

Seven didn't have the impression the little man was being honest, but decided that pressing further would likely see him at the bottom of lake Michigan with his feet in a block of concrete. "The guy in the red corner is yours, right?"

"That's right, Chuck Dempsey. No relation to the Manassa Mauler. I picked up this kid about two years back brawling with some of my boys in an alleyway. He knocked out three guys cold and broke another guy's nose. Chucky D's my top boy now."

"Sure. He's going to lose though. The other guy's got a mean straight and a good ten centimeters reach on him. Your guy's going to tire himself out trying to get close enough to connect one of those hooks you're so proud of. Tell his trainer to have him switch to southpaw. The blue guy's never fought a leftie before and he won't be able to wind up his straight anymore."

Caesar squinted his eyes at Seven and then at the boxers down below. Finally, he waved to Ajax. Ajax nodded and a minute later an old man in a white sweatshirt with a towel draped around his neck looked up towards the box with a baffled expression. In the next round he delivered the new instructions and the young fighter complied.

For the next two rounds Chucky D tossed strong jabs around until his opponent had tired himself out enough to slip up and try to dodge a blow by moving to the fighter's left. All Chucky D had to do was shift back to his normal orthodox stance and follow-up with a heavy punch to the man's jaw. Blue went down hard and didn't get back up.

Caesar flashed Seven a wide grin, one shiny golden tooth sparkling. "Not bad, Sinclair. Not bad at all. You like boxing?"

"Love it," lied the android. Everything he knew about the sport he had learned over the course of the last 15 minutes. He'd have to decide whether to keep all that knowledge or free up the few terabytes of memory later.

"Well, look at that. You could learn a thing or two from this guy, Ajax. How would you like a backstage tour, Sinclair?"

"That would be swell."

Chapter 28

Ajax led Seven downstairs to the training area. The detective could hear the distant roar of the crowd behind him. Ahead of him he could hear the sounds of gloved hands striking mats, rattling chains, and various masculine grunts that could have been from a workout or from constipation.

A scanner identified Ajax approaching and a metal sliding door opened, instantly intensifying the sounds. On the other side was a fully equipped gym with weights and dumbbells, punching bags, practice rings, you name it. It was a full house with at least two dozen athletes training for their turn to shine out in the big ring.

"Here we are," stated Ajax, taking one step into the room and one to the side and then going no further.

"I thought you were going to give me the grand tour," said Seven.

"No, Lloyd will show you around this area. I called ahead."

Right on cue, a muscular man with skin the color of good quality chocolate approached. His forehead was damp, and his t-shirt was dark from wetness under the arms and in a thick line down the center of his chest.

"Hey, you must be Seven, right? I'm Lloyd." He extended a hand wrapped with white tape. Seven shook it and gave it back to him. "Come on, I'll show you around."

Seven followed the man into the heart of the gym while Ajax remained exactly in the spot where he had left him. Ajax's only motion was in his neck as he rotated it to follow Seven's progress around the room.

In the center of the gym a terrified man was hanging upside down by his feet while a heavyweight threw jabs into his belly. The human punching bag screamed and attempted to shield himself with his arms rather unsuccessfully. The heavyweight didn't appear to be enjoying his workout.

"I'd like to see the job posting for that," commented Seven to his guide.

"Oh, that…" said Lloyd in a serious tone. "He's one of Caesar's soldiers. He got caught skimming a little off the top of some shipments. Caesar doesn't take too kindly to that."

"If that's what he does to friends I'd hate to be his enemy." Seven supposed the guy could at least count himself lucky that the heavyweight wore thick training gloves and was pulling his punches.

"Yes, you would. But don't worry about that. It sounded like Caesar has taken a shine to you. Come on, I wanna show you something."

Lloyd led the detective across the room to the training rings, which looked basically the same as the big ring the masses were watching outside, except that the men and women using these ones wore their normal workout clothing and protective headgear.

Lloyd went to a cabinet against the wall and picked up a black rectangular object and handed it to Seven. "Check this out."

The android examined the object briefly. It was a case, so he opened it. Inside was a pair of glasses that looked no different from a pair of reading spectacles.

"Go on, put them on and step into the ring."

Seven obliged to satisfy the man. Lloyd stretched the ropes for him and he entered the ring. The detective took one last look at the glasses and then placed them on his head. Now he was a robot wearing reading glasses. A sillier sight was probably hard to come by.

Suddenly another man appeared in the ring wearing his gloves and mouthpiece. The man lunged towards Seven with a fury as fast as if he had a jetpack on and he threw his fist hard into Seven's face…and it passed straight through. The man continued to throw a flurry of jabs and combinations at the android to little effect.

"Cute," said Seven.

"Aw, normally when I show people they freak out and fall on their butts. I guess you knew it was just augmented reality though."

"Nobody moves that silently. And the ring was empty before I put the glasses on."

"Yeah, makes shadowboxing way easier though."

"I can imagine," said Seven as he climbed back out of the arena.

Seven looked around the room and said, "Pretty sweet setup you got here. I bet this place has got some history too."

"Oh yeah, a lot of great stuff has come out of the Coliseum since Caesar had it built, and not just boxers either. They held the Super Bowl here a few years back when the Bears were in it. And they had the Republican National Convention here three times. We got a trophy case if you want to see it."

"I would, thanks," said Seven, glad that the man had suggested it for him.

The boxer led him to the other end of the room where a big glass case filled with plaques and trophies stood. Seven didn't care about them. He feigned interested for a minute and then turned his attention to the photographs hanging on the wall. Most were in digital frames, some even with moving pictures, but there were a few old fashioned paper photos as well from back in the days of Caesar's youth.

Seven examined each picture, taking note of every face and trying to guess their connection to the mobster. A grand opening ceremony, Caesar posing with his athletes and their trainers, Caesar shaking hands with the mayor, an ancient woman celebrating her 86th birthday, a wedding between two young people.

"Who's this?" Seven asked, pointing to the photo of the old woman.

"Caesar's ma."

"And this?" The detective pointed to the wedding photo.

"The fine lady there is Caesar's niece I think. His sister's daughter."

There were a lot of people visible in the photo. One in particular caught Seven's eye. There was a teenager in the background, probably no more than 15 years old, grinning like he was the one getting married. There was something familiar about his face. "How long ago was this taken?"

"Oh I dunno, maybe 10 to 15 years ago. Why?"

"A friend of mine is looking for a good wedding photographer."

"Ah, well I could ask around if you want."

"Don't bother. Looks like a nice family. Who are the people in the background?"

Seven became aware of Ajax's piercing gaze from across the room. The robot hadn't moved, but the detective had the feeling that his gaze had somehow intensified.

Lloyd replied, "Oh I wouldn't know that. Probably relatives of the groom though since I don't recognize any of them."

Seven nodded politely and then turned away from the photo. "Say, were you here last night by any chance?"

"Sure, why?"

"Do you know if anyone came to visit Caesar?"

Ajax moved suddenly for the first time since their arrival. He floated across the room with an uncanny grace for a man made of metal. He spoke to particularly large brute who was throwing his punching bag almost to the ceiling.

Lloyd looked thoughtful. "A lot of people come to see him, but nobody out of the ord—wait, there was his nephew, at least I think that's what he is. I don't see him around here very often. Why do you want to know?"

"Well it's a funny story, but to sum it up, a guy in a bar left his computer behind, and when I ran out to give it back to him I saw him get into a cab and drive away. A buddy of mine down at the Chicago PD says the cab drove to the Coliseum. I was hoping I'd find him here so I could return it to him."

"Oh, well that's nice of you. Most people would just keep it I guess."

"I'm not most people. What does this nephew look like?"

"I've only seen him a couple times. Blonde hair, blue eyes. Good looking young fellow." Lloyd put a finger on his lower lip, thinking, and then chuckled. "Huh, I don't even know his name now that I think about it. I saw him come in once with his girlfriend maybe two weeks ago."

"What did she look like?"

"I'm not sure I remember that. I think she had dark hair, or wait, was it blonde like his? I just saw them from a distance though."

"Could you ID them from a photo?"

"Uh, sure, I guess so, why—Oh hey Mike, what are you—"

Seven turned to see who had distracted his conversation partner. It was something huge, round, and red, and it was on a direct course for his face. This time the punch didn't pass gently through. It struck him hard and something loose rattled in Seven's head which had no business doing that. Seven's vision feed cut out and for about 10 milliseconds all he could hear was static.

The detective's vision returned almost a full second after his hearing. He was on the ground now. A massive gloved fist that looked like a plush lobster claw angled down towards him. Seven rolled to the side while Lloyd shouted something in confusion. The fist collided with the ground hard enough that the android could still feel it. Seven was still disoriented, but he managed to bring himself to his knees just in time to see that huge glove coming his way again. This time Seven made a fist of his own and hurled it into the red object. Something broke. It was a terrible cracking sound like an old, dry tree splitting. The big man's arm wasn't shaped like it used to be anymore and it was starting to turn purple.

"What the hell is going on here?" demanded Lloyd with fear in his white eyes.

Ajax stepped forward and addressed Seven. "What did I tell you about family matters?"

"That you can't discuss them or anything else. Thanks for the tour guys, it's been a real interactive experience, but it's getting late. I think I ought to be getting home now."

"No," replied Ajax in his calm voice. "It is too late for that now." The android snapped his fingers and a small army of muscles gathered at his flanks.

CHAPTER 29

Rizzo couldn't believe it. He was actually playing the errand boy for a robot now. Wasn't this exactly what they made the robots for? A day ago he would have laughed in the face of any guy who predicted he would be taking orders from a machine.

"I'm losing my mind," said the detective to himself while he sat in his car. He shook his head.

"I'm sorry, did you say something?" the vehicle asked politely.

"Can it," barked the detective.

He stared idly out his window at the dark city as it blurred by. Dark was something of an overstatement. All around him bright light poured out of windows and neon signs glowed. The clouds up above didn't want any of it so they flung it back down.

The university campus was alive and thirsty just like every Friday night. Youths already trudged along, staggering like the walking dead. Girls traveled in packs, dressed for the wrong season. Music blared loud enough that the detective could even hear it from inside his car.

It had taken him almost an hour to trace Grayson's corpse to the U of C Department of Pathology. It should have taken five minutes. Someone had forgotten to put it into the system, and the one guy who knew anything had gone home an hour before Rizzo called. Organization was clearly not his department's strong suit. Things like that gave him a bad itch. Sometimes he had the feeling he was working with idiots, and the rest of the world wasn't any better. Sometimes he wondered if that was a sign that there was something wrong with him.

"We are arriving at your destination," the car informed him. "Your destination is 50 meters straight ahead and to the left."

"Good. Wait for me here."

Rizzo climbed out of his wheeled palanquin and trod down the sidewalk, unconsciously counting the little grey circles left behind by the cadavers of old forsaken pieces of gum. The sliding door opened at his approach and he was greeted by a shiny white robot.

"Good evening, sir," said the robot. It held its hands lightly clasped in front of it like some robeless monk. "It is currently outside of normal operating hours. Unless you are here for a medical emergency I'm afraid I'll have to ask you to come again tomorrow between 7 a.m. and 8 p.m. I apologize for any inconvenience."

"There's no emergency," said Rizzo. He flashed his badge and explained, "I'm here on official police business. I need the personal effects of one of the bodies in your morgue. If you could just bring me there—"

"I'm sorry, but I'm afraid I'm not authorized to do that."

"Well who is?"

"Dr. Cheng is on duty this evening. Shall I call her?"

Rizzo sighed. "Yes, do that." He dropped himself into a chair before the robot had the chance to suggest it. It seemed like nearly every time he spoke to one of these machines he ended up waiting for a person to come.

About 15 minutes later, a tired, thin young woman in a white coat entered with a flat nose like she had walked into a wall and a high forehead that made her face look freakishly small. She looked like she had better things to do than talk to some cop at an hour before midnight.

"Can I help you?"

"I hope so. A body was brought here Tuesday night. I need to collect his belongings. They may be relevant for my investigation."

"Is it really necessary to do it right now in the middle of the night?"

"Sorry, but I'd rather not wait."

Dr. Cheng sighed and said, "Okay fine. I can bring you there. Come on. Wait, did you sign in with Gus already?"

"Who?"

"I'm Gus," stated the robot. "I have made note of your name. May I retain this information?"

"Yeah, yeah," groaned Rizzo impatiently.

It just occurred to him then that he had never noticed Seven asking anyone about permission to be remembered. Was the android somehow not compliant with privacy regulations? He supposed it shouldn't be too surprising, after all, the robot had hacked a police network to orchestrate a jailbreak.

"Okay, follow me," instructed the doctor.

Rizzo followed her through the winding corridors, passing through a few wards along the way. The majority of the personnel were robots. It was a quiet night.

Finally, they reached the morgue. It was a nice big room with enough space to dance a tango and enough beds to take a nap afterwards. The residents were quiet and kept to themselves. A nervous man with big curly golden hair shuffled towards them. His head looked like it would be great for sweeping a chimney.

"I'll leave you here with Mr. Wallace, okay?" asked the doctor. She left before Rizzo had the chance to answer.

"Mr. Wallace, I presume?" Rizzo asked the man. The detective looked him down and up. His socks were bright red with thin purple stripes. He was wearing a white lab coat, but the doctor hadn't given him a title. Some kind of technician probably. He had a white ear bud shoved in his right ear and a faint tapping sound like miniature drums emanated from it.

"Yes, what brings you here this time of day?" His forehead was shiny with sweat. "Heh, you're not as pale as my usual customers."

Rizzo ignored the bad quip and drew his badge. "I'm Sergeant Rizzo. On Tuesday night the body Miles Grayson was brought here. I'm here to pick up his personal effects. They're still here, right?"

Wallace looked surprised. "They are. You should thank me actually."

"Why's that?"

"A lady came here—," he glanced at his watch, "—about four hours ago wanting to collect his stuff. She claimed she was the widow and said she called the station to get the address here. I didn't give it to her though because I never got the okay from you guys to release the body or the stuff that came with it. She wasn't happy." He frowned and a hint of anger blew across his face like sand over the desert, and just as quickly it was gone leaving only barren terrain. "She threatened to stuff me into one of those." He indicated the row of square metal doors along the wall.

Rizzo pursed his lips. Clearly this lady had better luck than he did finding out where the body was. "What did she look like?"

"Tall, blonde, lot of plastic surgery."

"Okay, good work. So could you get that stuff for me then?"

"Yeah sure. Just a sec." He scurried off and returned a minute later with a small plastic, vacuum-sealed bag.

Rizzo took the bag and turned it over in his hands. "Is this all of it?"

Wallace flinched. "Yeah, of course."

"I see a shirt, pants, shoes... where's the suit coat? He was wearing one when we found him."

"I-it should all be in there."

"Where's the manifest?"

The technician hesitated for a moment and then said, "Wait, let me check something quick. I'll be back in a second." He sped away again and returned just a second later, as he had promised. He was holding a black sport coat. "I found this in the back. Maybe it, uh, got separated."

Rizzo yanked it from his hand with a wide sweeping motion. Wallace flinched, blinking hard, the fluff ball on top of his head jiggling. "Is this all of it now?"

"Yes, of cou—"

"Don't 'yes of course' me. You already said that before and it was a lie. Is this everything?"

"It is, I swear!"

Rizzo shook his head angrily. "If every idiot could just keep hands to himself and his money in his own damned pocket for just one day I swear it would be a miracle."

"S-sorry," said Wallace with a cracking voice like a pubescent teenager.

When Rizzo was younger he might have brought up charges against the man for theft, but at this point he had given up. All it brought was a lot of paperwork, but it didn't change anything. He wondered if that meant he was corrupt too now. He knew deep down that most cops didn't become corrupt for the money but because the system forced them to. You either swam with the current or you drowned. Rizzo was a good swimmer but he was getting old and tired.

Rizzo's phone started buzzing in his pocket. He shifted Grayson's junk into his other hand and drew the phone. He didn't recognize the number, but he answered anyway.

"What?" he barked more harshly than he normally would have.

"Hey, it's me," answered a guttural voice.

"Seven?"

"Right."

"How'd it go?" asked the officer in a calmer tone.

"Pretty good."

"Did you find anything?"

"Maybe. Nothing concrete though. Say, where are you right now?"

"At the university. I just picked up Grayson's things. Why?"

"How fast could you be at the 31st street beach?"

"Uh, maybe ten minutes."

"Great, meet me there in ten minutes. I'll be out on the pier. Don't be late. By the way, you've got your gun on you, right?"

"Yeah, I always do when I'm on duty. Why?"

"No reason. See you soon."

Rizzo pulled up outside of the beach and his vehicle informed him that it couldn't bring him any closer. The detective exited and continued on foot wondering why the robot would want to meet here of all places.

It was freezing cold, and the squall coming from the lake made his face hurt. He was following the footpath towards the pier when he spotted a group of three men struggling to carry something heavy. A robot holding a black plastic trash bag walked alongside them.

"What's that robot up to?" Rizzo asked himself. He tried to shove his hands deeper into his pockets but they didn't grow any bigger.

"Seven?" Rizzo called out as loud as he could.

The robot turned its head, but the three men weren't able to hear him over the wind. The robot either didn't recognize him or didn't feel like waiting.

Rizzo tried to get closer, fighting against the fierce gust. As he drew nearer he could see that the robot had an antenna sticking out from the top of its head. That clearly wasn't Seven. And the object the three men were carrying almost looked like a person.

The detective drew his pistol and fixed it on the three men. "Freeze! Police!"

All four turned their heads sharply in his direction. One of them looked back down at the thing between them and said, "You called the cops?" He lifted his foot and banged it into the object, producing a low clank.

Rizzo suddenly realized what the object they were carrying was. It was Seven, and the android's legs were bound together with a thick layer of duct tape. Silver tape spanned across the machine's silver chest, binding its arms to its torso.

"Drop it," ordered Rizzo.

The robot with the antenna said, "We are here on official business from Caesar." The words were uttered as if that made it a whole different story.

"I don't care if you're here on orders from the Pope. I said drop it."

They continued walking out the pier.

"You should really listen to him," said a voice that sounded like Seven.

"Shyaddup," snapped one of the men.

"Really. Don't you know who that is? That's Sergeant Antonio Rizzo, the mafia's bane, the scourge of all wrongdoers in Chicago. Every gangster in town fears his name. You guys are gangsters, right?"

The three men exchanged a nervous glance.

"Ignore him," ordered the robot with the antenna. It looked like a big handicapped bug with that ridiculous solitary little stick growing on its metal skull.

Rizzo shouted, "If I have to say it again it'll come with a bullet to make sure it sticks. Drop it and go back to wherever you crawled out from under."

"He wouldn't shoot us over a robot, would he?" asked the man who had kicked Seven earlier.

"That robot is part of an ongoing investigation," said Rizzo. "If I have to shoot you for obstruction of justice then so be it."

"I forgot my gat back at the Coliseum, guys," said one of the men, loosening his grip on Seven's feet.

The others nodded and one said, "Yeah, this ain't worth the hassle over some stupid tin can. No offense, Ajax."

Having reached an agreement, the men dropped their load without any regard for a soft landing. The three thugs turned and started to walk away, giving Rizzo a wide berth.

The robot with the antenna lingered for a moment, almost looking frustrated. Finally, it said, "Let this be a lesson to you. There will be no third chance." It dropped the trash bag and followed its human companions.

Rizzo stared at the robot with the antenna, struggling with a dilemma. This robot was what he had actually been expecting when he began this case. This robot was his proof that this technology is no good. It wasn't too late to catch it before it escaped. Finally, with great effort, he turned away, resolving to stay focused on one thing at a time.

Rizzo hurried to Seven's side, holstering his gun and pulling out a small pocket knife from his pocket. He sawed through the duct tape on Seven's arms and legs.

"What's the matter with you?" shouted Rizzo angrily. "Why didn't you tell me you were in trouble on the phone?"

"I figured if I did you'd call for backup," replied Seven, peeling tape off his body.

"Of course I would have. That's exactly why you should have told me."

"You'd have called for backup and then I would have ended up back in a cell. I'm still wanted for murder in case you've forgotten."

"I've half a mind to put you in a cell right now."

"I'm going to be sticky for days," said the robot glumly, picking at clumps of adhesive on its chest.

Seven walked over to the fallen trash bag and ripped it open. The robot pulled out its hat and coat and restored them to their proper place.

Rizzo sighed. "Would it kill you to at least say thanks?"

"Probably not, but better safe than sorry."

"Nobody likes a smartass."

"Did you get the stuff?"

"Yeah," grumbled Rizzo. "It's in the car."

"Good. Let's go someplace quiet and catch each other up."

CHAPTER 30

Rizzo sat across from Seven in a burger joint downtown that was open 24 hours. The light inside was too bright and the music coming from the kitchen was too loud. They were the only customers, and had already been there for 15 minutes. The waitress sitting behind the counter saw them come in but seemed disinterested.

The grey man still couldn't believe it. He couldn't remember having ever spent so much time with a robot before. He hated technology and probably always would, but despite his best efforts he had to admit that the android fascinated him. The machine was probably as big a pain in the backside as he was and somehow he liked that.

Finally, the waitress seemed to decide she ought to do something for her wages. She stood up and sauntered over to their table chewing something like a cow chews cud. The woman's entire being screamed that she didn't want to be there. She stopped abruptly at the detectives' table, thrust her hip to one side, and poised a hand to rest her weight on that protruding pelvis.

"What'll it be, boys?"

"Coffee," said Rizzo. "Black."

"A damp cloth for me," said Seven.

The waitress let her hand slip from her hip. Her mouth melted and her eyes held an expression of dull disgust.

"Not to eat," clarified the android. It pointed to its sticky chest which was already beginning to accumulate grime from the sooty air outside. "I'm dirty."

"Whatever," said the waitress rolling her eyes. She turned and walked away again.

"So what happened at the Coliseum?" Rizzo asked once the waitress was out of earshot.

"I talked to Caesar—"

"You talked to Caes—" Rizzo said loudly in surprise before catching himself and repeating more quietly, "You talked to Caesar? Directly? In person?"

"Yep."

"How?"

"A magician never reveals his secrets."

"How old are you?" asked Rizzo grumpily.

"Six years, 49 days, 12 hours, 3 minutes, and 21 seconds."

"Practically a toddler. That explains a lot."

"That wasn't nice," said the robot. Rizzo almost felt guilty. "Anyway I talked to him and he denied any knowledge or involvement."

"Do you believe him?"

"Not for a second. He definitely knows something. For a seasoned criminal he's a poor liar. Plus his lackey, Ajax, tried to give me a one-way ticket to Atlantis. Why bother if he's really not involved in any way?"

"Isn't Atlantis in the Atlantic?"

"Remind me which of us is the smartass."

Rizzo smiled, and his moustache tickled his lower lip.

The robot continued, "While I was getting the grand tour of his gym—"

"You got a tour too?" Rizzo was impressed. It was uncanny how much these last few hours reminded him of those two weeks he worked with Vic Sinclair way back when.

"If I didn't I wouldn't have said it. I'd like to finish my story now if that's all right with you."

"Yeah, yeah. I won't interrupt again. Go on."

"So while a guy was showing me around I asked him if anyone interesting showed up last night and he mentioned some nephew of Caesar's being there who doesn't normally visit. While I was digging for details Ajax, that robot you saw earlier, noticed me asking too many questions and had a tank with arms knock me down.

"I have to ask myself, why did a little bit of innocent digging get Ajax's panties all up in a bunch if there was nothing there? Why was he even keeping such a close eye on me at all? If they really didn't want me to learn anything, why give me a tour at all? And even if they just wanted to keep up appearances, Ajax could have been the one to show me around, but instead he passed me on to someone else while he watched. It was almost as if they wanted to see how much I knew or how much I suspected.

"And another thing. Caesar even tried to deny having ever even heard the name Grayson. Can it be that a businessman like Caesar really doesn't know one of the most powerful men in the city? I don't think so. Someone is clearly hiding something."

The waitress dawdled over to the table carrying a little tray in one hand and a wet rag between two fingers in the other. She held out the rag in front of Seven and let it drop onto the table with a comical splat, spreading tiny droplets over the table and on the android. She took a small white mug off the tray and set it down in front of Rizzo and then wordlessly walked back to the counter where she tossed the tray aside. In one seamless motion, she pulled her phone out of her apron, held it in front of her face, and sat down on a stool. It looked like a maneuver trained with years of practice.

The robot took the rag and began a fruitless effort to remove the dirty adhesive from its chest. Rizzo watched with something between amusement and wonder. It was uncanny how human the android looked in that moment.

"You think this nephew might be our masked man?" asked Rizzo.

"Could be," replied Seven without looking up.

"Did you get a name?"

"No, the guy I talked to probably wouldn't have known it, but I didn't really get the chance to ask."

"Well, it's something at least" said Rizzo after taking a sip of his coffee. It tasted like someone had put dirt in the filter instead of coffee grind. "By the way, I also learned something while picking up Grayson's stuff."

The sergeant waited for some kind of acknowledgement from the robot until it became awkward, but none ever came. He frowned and continued, "Apparently his wife was there a few hours before me wanting his things too. It was pure luck that we were able to get it first. If we would have waited until tomorrow she might have gotten the station to issue clearance to release the body."

Still meticulously scrubbing, Seven said, "Mmm, she's a sentimental woman."

"That's sarcasm, right? I've met the lady. When I told her that her husband was dead she practically wet herself laughing."

Seven set the wash cloth down on the corner of the table and looked up, apparently having given up with the cleanse. The android looked at the small pile on the bench beside Rizzo and said, "So let's see this stuff you picked up."

Rizzo set it in the middle of the table, curious to see what the robot expected to find.

Seven took the plastic package and ripped open the vacuum seal. The machine proceeded to scrutinize each item as if it were covered with some microscopic text. It examined each shoe and each sock. It scanned the pants, turning out each pocket, front and back. Even the boxer shorts were examined in detail.

Finally, Seven set aside the items which had been wrapped and picked up the coat from the table. The android emptied the inside pockets and seemed to be captivated by a shiny metallic black stylus pen. It was a particularly nice pen, and knowing the man who had been carrying it, Rizzo could imagine it cost more than it had any right to. The metal man sat motionless with the pen between its thumb and forefinger for so long that Rizzo began considering the possibility that the machine had frozen when suddenly it placed the pen in its own coat pocket.

"Hey, that's evidence!" protested Rizzo.

"I'll give it back," said Seven calmly.

"Now wait just a minute," said the older man firmly. He used that same tone when his daughter was misbehaving. "These items are my responsibility, and I'm not letting them out of my sight for a second. Put it back now."

"No."

"Wha—"

"Do you want to know who killed Grayson?"

"You mean you know who did it?" asked Rizzo, slightly disoriented by the sudden jump in topics. He wondered if the android was trying to trick him now.

"I believe I do, but it's too late to do anything tonight. We'll need to wait until morning."

"Wait for what?"

"I think it's time we have ourselves a little get-together. We'll gather all the players together in one place and find our answers once and for all."

"I thought you said you knew who killed Grayson already."

"I do, but I'm not 100 percent sure why yet or how everything was arranged."

"Why don't you just tell me what you know and we'll figure it out together."

The android shook its head. "No, I don't like that plan. We'll go with mine. Tomorrow morning I'll call Max Kaminski and Elizabeth Grayson and tell them to meet me at Sophie Harper's place. She's got a nice big clean house in a quiet neighborhood. It's a good place for a party."

"And what do you expect me to do?" asked Rizzo realizing it would be an exercise in futility to try to argue with a machine. He took another sip of that dirt water in his mug and for the life of him could not fathom why he had done that.

"I need you to hide in a place where you can watch the house until our masked friend makes his appearance."

"What makes you think he'll show up?"

"He will."

Rizzo sighed a deep sigh wondering why he was still going along with this circus instead of just arresting the robot. Curiosity, he supposed.

"You should go home and get some sleep," said Seven, standing up. "I'll call you in the morning once everything is arranged. You can stay in contact with me using the number I called from tonight. Normally I rotate it daily, but I'll leave it for you. You're welcome."

CHAPTER 31

A thin ray of light stabbed its way through the thick grey clouds on Saturday morning. Today was the day the sun would make its move. Today it would finally break through that dark veil and let the city bask in its warmth. At least that's what it told itself. The weatherman had something else to say about it.

It was a calm, quiet morning in Sophie Harper's neighborhood. It had just rained an hour before, and the air still carried that fresh rain smell, and the earthworms were struggling not to drown in it. Seven had to sidestep on a few occasions on his way down the path from the street to the house to avoid stepping on the little invertebrates. Upon reaching the door he poked a finger into the little button mounted on the wall and waited for the door to open.

Seven stood perfectly still and waited patiently for just under five minutes until the door finally opened. When it did open, it did so ever so slightly, just enough for the girl to peek out with one eye. She had a camera on the door, so it was a senseless act, but Seven knew that humans often insisted on seeing things directly.

"Morning Sophie," greeted the android cheerfully. He waited for another 60 seconds while the girl stood there frozen.

"H-hi," she said weakly, opening the door slightly further.

Seven took a step forward and pushed the door open, causing the girl to squeak in alarm. He walked past her into the house without bothering to watch her close the door behind him.

"Hey," she said in a tone firmer than he expected her to possess. "You can't just barge in here. I...You can't just barge in here."

"If you say it a third time maybe it'll be true."

"I'm going to call the police if you don't leave right now," said the girl stomping her little foot. She was wearing a thin, white dressing gown which went down to her shins. Two pink flannel legs continued from there down to the fluffy white bunny-shaped slippers on her feet.

"Oh, did I forget to mention that I'm working with the police now? Turns out there was a little mix-up down at the station all this time. I guess somebody just wanted it to look like I was guilty. Detective Rizzo set everyone back on track though. You've met the good detective, right? He'll be joining us in a bit. But right now I suggest you get yourself dressed and ready for our guests."

"Wha...guests?" asked the girl sleepily.

"It's a noun: a person who is invited to visit someone's home or to attend a particular social occasion. From Middle English 'gest', from Old Norse 'gestr'. No wonder Grayson didn't like your reports if you're missing basic vocabulary like this."

Sophie stared at him dumbly, her lips slightly parted like they couldn't decide whether or not they should do something. Seven ignored her and sat down on the couch. He had warned her that there would be visitors; it was her choice whether she wanted to receive them in her pajamas or not.

Sophie disappeared into the downstairs bathroom for 6 minutes, and then spent the next 15 wandering around, always seeming like her goal suddenly shifted just before she started to do something. Then the doorbell rang and the girl squeaked again and nearly jumped out of the bunnies sucking on her feet.

"I'll get it," said Seven, already on his way to the door.

The android opened up without bothering to see who it was on the display. Max Kaminski stood in the doorway wearing relatively clean jeans and a white button shirt under his coat. He had some gel or hairspray in his hair that made it seem like he had dunked his head into some kind of laminate.

"Morning Maxi," greeted Seven. He stepped aside to invite the programmer inside, and like a good host he took the man's coat and hung it on one of the pegs beside the door.

"You said something about introducing me to BlackAlice," said Kaminski.

"Patience."

Sophie stood in the hallway with a look of horror in her eyes.

Kaminski grinned wide when he saw the girl and whispered to Seven, "Is she her? Is she BlackAlice?"

"Keep it in your pants, stud. We're not all present yet."

Seven ushered Kaminski into the living room and placed him on the sofa. "Max, this is Sophie Harper. Sophie, this is Max Kaminski."

"H-hi," said Sophie, looking around nervously in case any more visitors suddenly appeared. Her ghastly pallor made the carpet look grey.

"Sup," said Kaminski in a poor attempt to seem cool. That was basically where the conversation ended. Neither human said another word for the next 10 minutes.

Then the doorbell rang once more and Seven answered it. A moment later he returned in the company of a tall blonde in her late 40s. When he came back the two young people were still sitting in silence where he had left them.

"If I can interrupt your captivating conversation for just a moment," said Seven, "I'd like to introduce you both to Mrs. Elizabeth Grayson. Beth, this is Sophie Harper and Max Kaminski. You may be happy to learn that Maxi here was the guy who slugged your late husband in his office."

Mrs. Grayson smiled weakly, an expression of humored patience. Kaminski looked like he was going to be sick.

"She's not…" said Kaminski, unable to finish the thought out loud.

"We're still not complete. Be patient."

Sophie seemed to find her voice again and asked irritably, "Just how many people are you bringing into my house?"

"Don't worry," assured Seven, "just two more."

He placed the older woman on a chair perpendicular to the couch and seated himself between Kaminski and Sophie. The next 15 minutes were awkward and uncomfortable for the three humans, who sat silently, uncertain what they should say to one another.

"You folks are about as lively as a funeral parlor," said Seven finally. He had hoped that the group might converse so that he could learn something about their relationships. "Max, how'd your interview go?"

"Oh," replied the programmer, glancing at Sophie and then turning red. "G-good. It went pretty well. I think they're gonna make me an offer."

"That's good news. Wouldn't you say so, Sophie?"

"Y-yes," replied the girl without looking up from the floor.

"And how about you, Beth?" continued the android. "Any luck getting your husband's body released?"

"How did you—no, not yet."

"That's too bad. Keep trying. Today's your lucky day. I can feel it."

Seven turned to Sophie next. "And what about you? You going back to work next we—"

Before he could finish his question, a startled cry resonated through the house, and the rustling sounds of struggle accompanied them. Seven stood up promptly and hurried towards the front door. In the entry hall, Rizzo was battling to subdue the familiar masked man. The detective was holding the man's wrists to his sides. His opponent was holding a gun in one hand.

Just as Seven arrived, the masked man planted a knee into Rizzo's belly, and the older detective crumpled. Before the masked assailant had an opportunity to do anything else, Seven was upon him. The android drove a metal fist into the center of the balaclava, and his target bounced off the wall and slid down to the floor.

Together, Rizzo and Seven laid the man face-down and while Rizzo tried to cuff him. It was no easy task since he was struggling and flailing like a caught fish.

"Max!" said Seven loudly with the best sense of urgency he was able to imitate. "Don't just sit there. Grab the gun."

Kaminski widened his eyes in horror, but he stood up obediently and approached the trio. The programmer bent over and grabbed the barrel of the pistol and pulled. With obvious effort, he finally managed to free it from the masked man's gloved hand.

Rizzo slapped his handcuffs around his attacker's wrists and then stood up, dragging the masked man to his feet. Breathing heavily, the old cop pushed the masked man into the living room at arm's length. The masked man had an angry fire in his eyes. He moved stiffly as if his joints needed to be oiled, but more likely out of a refusal to walk.

Kaminski stood there holding the gun out in front of him like it might be radioactive. Rizzo snatched it out of his hand and pocketed it as he passed.

The sergeant looked at Seven and said, "So he was here, just like you predicted. How'd you know he'd show up?"

"Call it a hunch." Seven looked around the room and announced, "Now that everyone is here we can begin. Mr. Rizzo, would you like to have the honor of unveiling our friend here?"

"It would be my pleasure," said the detective, taking a handful of black cloth from the top of the masked man's head and then pulling. Beneath the mask was a ruffled mess of sandy blonde hair with a handsome face attached to it. It was the face of Ethan Willis. A red blood smear had formed beneath his left nostril.

Rizzo looked startled, and Sophie placed a hand over her mouth. Kaminski looked clueless and Mrs. Grayson looked amused.

"Did you know it was Willis?" asked Rizzo.

"I wasn't certain," replied Seven. "I had already considered it even before the murder based on the eyes, but I was never able to get a clear retina scan from the masked man. I was 70% sure it was him after visiting Caesar. Willis is the brother of Casesar's niece's husband. I recognized him in a family photo in the Coliseum gym.

"You traced the masked man's cab to the Coliseum Thursday night where I assume he tried to get help from his sister-in-law's uncle. I can only assume the mobster declined.

"I thought it was a pretty strange coincidence that Grayson would turn up dead the very same day someone hired me to investigate him. There never was any theft, or bitbucks either, was there? It was just an excuse to get some poor sap there at the crime scene so you could pin it on him. Why'd you do it?"

Willis snarled but didn't speak.

"You committed murder and then tried to pin it on me. Plus you shot a cop. All for what, some petty grudge because Grayson didn't want to play nicely?"

"You don't understand," protested Willis. "With Speculo's technology we could have changed the world. We could have replicated any kind of matter in the universe at almost no cost. Gold and silver would be no different than iron or copper. Think of how it would revolutionize the tech industry, the automotive industry, the medical industry. There would be no need for organ donors or artificial replacements anymore; we could simply generate a new heart or kidney at the snap of a finger. With this technology we could solve world hunger." Willis bared his teeth and concluded, "The only thing standing in my way was Miles Grayson."

"Mmm, and now you're going to prison. So much for that."

Rizzo frowned, still holding Willis by the cuffs. "In case you forgot, Willis has an airtight alibi. I looked into it myself and it checks out."

"Indeed," agreed Seven. "Willis is not the killer. Or at least, he's not the one who pulled the trigger. You can argue semantics about whether he's still the killer or not later."

"Then who did pull the trigger?"

"She did," said Seven, pointing his chin at Sophie.

This time everyone was shocked, and for a moment even Elizabeth Grayson forgot to be amused. Sophie hid her face in her hands.

"I'm confused," said Kaminski slowly.

"That's okay," said Seven. "You're not alone."

"I was with you up till now," said Rizzo looking concerned. "You'd better have a good explanation if you're going to drop a bomb like that."

"I do. She knew Willis by name which struck me as odd, so I checked around. Nobody in her department or in IT seemed to have heard of him before, and I read through the reports on Grayson's desk related to Speculo, and she was not involved in that project. And, of course, I saw that." The android gestured towards the painting on the wall.

Recognition suddenly registered on Rizzo's face. "The paintings! I knew I had seen something like it before when I was here on Thursday night. The paintings at Speculo were made by the same artist."

"Exactly, and that artist was Sophie. Ethan Willis is Sophie's boyfriend."

"This is ridiculous," said Willis. "I've never seen this woman before."

"Well we already know that's a lie," said Seven. "You were here Thursday night. Want to try again?"

The android looked at Sophie who was still covering her eyes as if that would make them all disappear. "You murdered Miles Grayson in his office on Tuesday night, didn't you Ms. Harper?"

"No!" she protested. "It's not true!" She repeated that sentence twice more, each time more quietly than the last.

"Care to explain why every time I was with you the masked man suddenly showed up? And each time, shortly before that you disappeared somewhere. In the alleyway you ran off to pick up your dropped ball because you knew Willis was going to attack me there. In the bar you disappeared into the bathroom to call him and warn him I was looking for him. In your house while I was scanning his computer you disappeared somewhere to tell him I was still there. And today you went into the bathroom shortly after I arrived where you called him again."

"No, no, no..." she said.

"All you have are a lot of meaningless words," snarled Willis. "You have no proof."

"Unfortunately he's right," agreed Rizzo.

"No, he's not," replied Seven.

Mrs. Grayson spoke up for the first time to say, "I'm sorry, this is all quite entertaining, but what does this all have to do with me?"

"Why, Mrs. Grayson, you're the one who solved the case."

Seven walked across the room and turned on the TV. He swiftly navigated through the menus to set up a connection to a Bluetooth device. He then established a link and a series of audio files appeared on the screen. The android selected one and pressed the play button.

"What do you want?" barked the voice of Miles Grayson through the speakers.

Silence.

"I asked you a question. What! What's the meaning of this?"

The voice of Sophie answered, "Do you know how long I've suffered under you?" Her voice was shaky and saturated with a bundle of mixed emotions. "Every report I've ever given you you've torn apart. Every single one. I was top of my class, you know. Valedictorian. I work overtime every day. I work harder and better than everyone in here, and what do I get for it? I get told that I'm worthless trash on a daily basis.

"But do you know what? That was okay. I was able to live with that. But then…then Ethan needed something from Orion, and I helped him talk to the right people and push his idea through, and then you came along yet again and pissed all over it like you always do. You're despicable."

"Are you finished?" asked the voice of Grayson. "Your monologues are even more bland than your reports. Put the gun away and crawl back into your office like a good little girl before you mess things up like usual and shoot yourself in the foot. The last thing I need right now is a bloodstain on my floor."

"I'm sorry, Mr. Grayson. I really am. I wish it didn't have to be this way."

"Get out of my—"

BANG! And that was the end of the clip.

All the fight went out of Willis's eyes, and Sophie's pallor gave a whole new meaning to the color white. Mrs. Grayson smiled.

"I thought you might get a kick out of that," said the android to Beth Grayson. Seven pulled the stylus pen out of his coat pocket and held it up between his thumb and forefinger. "This little guy is actually a listening device. Mrs. Grayson was using it to spy on her husband and scoop up the dirt to use in her divorce trial."

"Is that why she wanted Grayson's belongings last night?" asked Rizzo. "But why? And why not just tell the police?"

"It wasn't exactly legal," she answered with a shrug. "And I didn't know what might be on it. I had a fight with my husband in his office earlier that day. I thought maybe it would be incriminating, so I wanted to look for myself first. How did you know what it was?"

"I was looking for it," said the android. "You seemed to have knowledge about a lot of things that went on inside your husband's office. Things which you probably shouldn't have known about like his fight with Kaminski here. I was suspecting a bug of some sort either in his office or on his person, and there it was. Thanks for that by the way.

"Grayson plowed through his brief existence living a hedonistic life full of wanton malice and debauchery, stomping on those weaker than himself like bugs. And it worked out pretty well for him until one of those little bugs turned out to be tougher than he thought. In the end, the Miles Grayson program encountered a fatal exception, an error he could not recover from." Seven addressed the whole group, turning to make eye contact with each of them, finally resting upon Sophie.

Some of the fire suddenly blazed back into Willis's blue eyes. "How can we be sure that audio clip is real? It could be fake."

"I'm the one who picked it up from the morgue last night," said the sergeant. "Grayson definitely had it on him when he died."

"But this robot can alter its voice. We all know it. It could have faked Sophie's voice. It could have even faked Grayson's voice for that matter."

"Sure," said Seven calmly, "I could have. But the timestamp on the audio clip matches up with the time of death, so if the pen was on Grayson when he died then I must have killed him and planted it on him. Makes sense except that in this scenario I'm apparently smart enough to frame Sophie with a hidden microphone but then accidentally framed myself by tampering with the security cameras.

"Did I forget to mention that bit? The video of me entering and leaving Grayson's office was copy pasted from my visit that afternoon, and apparently somebody tried to bribe forensics to keep quiet about it. I'm guessing uncle Caesar helped set that one up. By the way, the cameras were also the entire reason for the masked assailant in that alleyway too, isn't that right? The first time I entered Grayson's office I passed by Sophie on my way in, so that footage couldn't be reused for the time of the murder at night without incriminating her. After murdering Grayson, Sophie logged onto the server where the video is stored using Kaminski's credentials and put her graphic design skills to good use doctoring that video feed."

Rizzo nodded, now seeing how it all fit together. "And then she used her own access to wipe the receptionist's memories."

Sophie sat on the couch with her elbows on her knees trying to squash her head with her palms. She looked like a war veteran reliving some past trauma in her head.

"Willis is already safely in our pockets for shooting a cop. Now as for little Miss Harper here, now that we know where to look I'm sure we can find some pretty interesting things if we dig deep enough. Maybe some incriminating emails, a copy of Max's rootkit, or maybe even the murder weapon."

"This is ridiculous," protested Willis in a pitch at least one notch higher than normal. "You're just a robot. You don't have any authority."

"No, but I do," said Rizzo, shaking the man slightly to remind him he was there.

Willis started to argue when Sophie said, "Stop." He did, and she took a long, deep breath. "It's true. All of it. I did it."

"Sophie…" said Willis pleadingly.

"I-I killed Mr. Grayson." She looked pretty dangerous in her pink pajamas and bunny slippers.

There was silence in the room for a moment until Kaminski shyly said, "I, uh, so then who is BlackAlice?"

"That's a good question," said Seven. "Which one of you is BlackAlice?"

"We took turns," spat Willis reluctantly. Kaminski's shoulders slumped, and his sad puppy dog eyes drifted down towards the floor.

Seven patted Kaminski on the back and said, "They social engineered you into giving up your credentials, pal. Plus that rather incriminating piece of malware you wrote. I don't know if that was the target or just an extra little goodie. But cheer up; at least you maybe got that job. I hope you learned something from this experience."

Rizzo pulled out his phone and called it in.

CHAPTER 32

On Monday morning, bright and early, Rizzo called Seven and asked him to meet him at that shabby diner where they had met on Friday night after Seven's close call with Caesar's brutes. The old detective was already sitting at the same booth when Seven arrived. Half the tables were occupied, and the waitress seemed slightly more motivated this time.

Seven sat down across from Rizzo.

"Thanks for coming," Rizzo said. "You seen the news?" He pointed at the TV hanging over the counter.

Seven turned his head to watch. It was a report about the recent capture of the murderers of the CFO of Orion Industries. The media seemed to be sensationalizing it, talking to various experts in the fields of economics, business, and psychology to examine the motives. The screen cut to a recording of an interview with Sergeant Rizzo who apparently single-handedly solved the case.

"Congratulations," said the robot flatly with no hint of emotion.

Rizzo frowned. "I feel a little bad for taking all the credit now. It was actually you who solved it."

"It's how it had to be."

"I was thinking about what I could do to make it even—"

"Thanks, but I'm fine."

"Shut up and let me finish before I change my mind," barked the cop grumpily. "Murphy, one of our forensics guys, owes me a favor. I'm going to ask him to delete everything in our system about your involvement in the case. I'm also going to ask him to set you up as a confidential informant, so if anyone does find out about your...uniqueness, you'll have a sort of immunity."

Seven sat there motionless, unblinking.

"You're welcome," said Rizzo slowly with a rising tone as if it were a question.

The waitress came to their table and asked, "What'll it be this time?"

"I'll have the bacon and eggs breakfast," said Rizzo.

"Coffee?"

"You know, I think I'll pass this time."

"And what about you?" she asked Seven. "You look like you've got an appetite today. Maybe a towel this time?"

"Nothing for me," said Seven.

The waitress shoved the device where she entered the orders into her apron and walked away.

The two sat in silence for a moment until Seven said, "This was my first big case without Vic." He wasn't sure why he said it. The sentence had no real purpose. It just seemed like the sort of thing a person might say.

"I think he would be proud."

Seven said nothing.

"By the way," said Rizzo with a goofy smile. "I've got something else for you. Here." He reached into a tan cloth tote bag sitting on the booth beside him and pulled out a white sheet of paper folded in half. He handed it to the android.

"That's a card from my daughter," explained the sergeant.

A colored pencil drawing on the front side depicted a smiling grey stick figure wearing a brown hat and a lighter brown coat standing on a green field. Crooked grey skyscrapers towered in the background on the left side. Floating at knee height above the grass beside the grey person was a pink blob with little black spots, four limbs, and a tail. Surprisingly detailed clouds padded the top quarter of the page. Even in a kid's drawing the sun couldn't catch a break. Seven opened the card and inside was scrawled in big multicolored letters the sentence 'so your not lonely'.

Before Seven could ask what it was supposed to mean, Rizzo reached into the tote bag and pulled out a little clear plastic box and set it on the table. At the bottom of the box was a layer of brown pea gravel with a little rock in the center and a fake plant in the corner. A small pale pink gecko about ten centimeters long with black-brown spots on its back was stuck to one of the plastic walls staring at the robot with huge black eyes that dominated its head.

"This is for you. After I told Abby about you she insisted. She was worried you'd be lonely. Kids, right? She picked the color."

"What am I supposed to do with it?"

"I don't know. Take it home and give it a name. Or give it away if you don't want it. What do I care? You know how to take care of a pet, right?"

Seven spent the next four seconds downloading a terabyte of owner's manuals and guides. "I do now." He stared at the little lizard. The kid's drawing hadn't been too far off from reality. It was a chubby little reptile with a round head. It was female.

"Is Vicky a good name?" Seven asked. He had never had to name something before.

Rizzo smiled and chuckled softly. "Sure. It's a good name."

The waitress brought Rizzo's breakfast, and the human began to consume it. The nearly black bacon made audible crunching sounds when he bit it.

"So what are you going to do now?" he asked the android casually.

"A little bit of this and a little bit of that."

"You really don't like to share, do you?"

"I can't tell you what comes next. It all depends on who walks through my door."

"Well I don't know about you, but I've got a ton of work to do while my partner is gone."

"As your new CI, if you need a hand you can always call. I offer a pretty fair rate," offered the robot.

"No. I'll pass on that. This has been more than enough technology for one week."

"Suit yourself. I suppose I ought to get going then if you're busy."

Seven stood up and Rizzo stood up with him. The cop seemed indecisive for a moment and then he extended a hand. Seven stared at it and then clasped it.

"It's been interesting," said Rizzo.

"Indeed."

"Don't forget your lizard," teased the old man with a smile.

"She's a gecko and her name is Vicky," said Seven, placing the plastic box back into the tote bag and taking it in his hand.

"Heh, sure," laughed Rizzo. "Well, I guess this is goodbye then. Stay out of trouble."

Seven unlocked the door to the Sinclair Detective Agency and stepped inside. Everything was exactly as he had left it. He had half expected it to have all been brought away to some dusty evidence room or that the cops would have left the door open and vandals would have ravaged the place. The lights came on as he entered.

The android carried Vicky's cage across the room to a table and cleared a space for her. He would need to buy a heating pad for the tank, and food. He started a thread to search for a good price online. Seven displayed the little girl's card beside the cage. He thought maybe his new pet might like some color. It was a pretty drab, colorless office.

He took off his hat and coat and placed them carefully on the rack in the corner and then seated himself at his desk. The android placed his palms flat on the table and sat like that perfectly still, waiting for something to happen.

Made in the USA
Las Vegas, NV
10 February 2022